Lynton,

The Karoo Vampire

And the Jewels Of

Omar Bin Abi

(Old Tales, New Twists)

#11 in the Series

By

J. Wayne Frye

Notice:
This book is written in Canadian English
and teachers should alert their students
to the variances in spellings.

TO:
Margaret and Aldo Porras - neighbours in
a golden time in a golden place.
Steve Epstein – my office mate from a hundred
years ago – we went our separate ways but found
each other again through modern technology. Our
audiences always said, "Frye has the charisma,
and Steve has the brains." Nothing has changed
after all this time!

E.R.B. and J.W.P for the inspiration

AND AS ALWAYS, TO MY MUSE
Lynton Viñas

Catalogue Number:
ISBN: 978-1-928183-28-0

Fireside Books – Canadian Division
Part of the Peninsula Publishing Consortium

TABLE OF CONTENTS

ABOUT THE AUTHOR

The author with the real-life Lynton Viñas

Wayne Frye's *Aaron Adams* mysteries, *Chablis Louise Chavez* thrillers, *Girl* books and *Lynton* adventures have titillated the brains of those who enjoy tantalizing tales that challenge the mind. His life, like the heroes he writes about, has been filled with adventure and excitement.

Wayne Frye has been a college hockey coach, university professor, and at one time, the youngest university president in the USA. Called a marketing genius by the LOS ANGELES TIMES, he has been a promotional consultant to hockey teams and motion picture companies. He has been cited for his work with inner-city gangs in the Los Angeles area and been active in the anti-globalization movement. He became a Canadian citizen in 2003 and lives in Ladysmith, British Columbia and Cavite, Philippines. He provides satirical political commentary to many Canadian newspapers, and his books on politics have created a great deal of controversy.

Some of the 42 books by J. Wayne Frye

Hockey Mania and the Mystery of Nancy Running Elk
Something Evil in the Darkness at Hopkins House
How Hockey Saved a Jew From the Holocaust
The Girl Who Stirred up the Whirlwind
The Girl Who Motivated Murder Most Foul
The Girl Who Said Goodbye for the Last Time
White Meteors and the Ghost of Sue Ann McGee
Fall From Apocalypse
Armageddon Now
Worth
When Jesus Came to Jersey as the Son of Thunder
When Jesus Came to Canada to Lead an Indigenous Rebellion
Canadian Angels of Mercy – Nurses in Times of Peril
Points of Rebellion: Aboriginals Who Fought for Justice
Lynton Walks on Water
Lynton Curls Her Hair
Lynton and the Vampire at Tagaytay Manor
Lynton Buys a Cell-Phone and Hears the Voice of Doom
Lynton and Beowulf in the Taal Inferno
Lynton and the Ghosts in the Mansion on Balete Drive
Lynton's South African Adventure
Chablis: Avenging Angel for the Forgotten
In the City of Lost Hope
Chablis and the Terrorist
Pursuit
The Disappearance

Prologue

Survival Instincts

"What bait do you use,"

Said a Saint to the Devil,

"When you fish where

The souls of people abound?"

"Well, for almost all tastes,"

Said the King of Evil,

"The lure of gold is the best I've found

In a world where greed rules supreme."

"Ah then," queried the Saint,

"You find the sparkle of gold

Sufficient to entice all

To bow before your bait?"

Said the Devil, "I angle for people's greed.

Rare are the few who refuse to bow,

But I can get them all eventually,

As the lure will grow from my evil seed."

Said the Saint back to the devil,
As he stirred a cauldron of hope,
"You need to peer in here
And meet the one you should fear."

The devil hesitated there for awhile.
He knew no person he should fear.
Then, he moved tepidly toward the Saint,
Wondering who could test evil's fate.

Ah, the devil gazed into the cauldron,
Where the image of a woman came into view.
The light of this angel did in him anger sow.
Alas, it was the image of the dynamic dynamo!

The world is a place that has always been controlled by the mighty. Being mighty does not necessarily mean having great physical attributes that make you able to subdue others with the force of superior strength. In modern times, strength can also come from the size of an individual's bank account in a world where financial assets are deemed the judge of a person's worth. It is not your character that counts, but the house in which you live, the car you drive, the Gucci bag you carry and the other expensive accouterments that make you stand above your fellow human being who must toil in obscurity to put food on the table. Whether an ancient warlord or despicable, money-grubbing modern captain of industry, the outcome in a world where greed is aggrandized as an enviable trait is always the same. Those born into privilege are to be exalted, while the rest of us swim in a shark-infested sea filled with the predators of capitalism.

Most of us born into modest means have grand dreams of being rich, because media ballyhoos the rewards of capitalism that makes it possible for every person to attain riches. In reality, that is a rarity, as generally, only those born into affluence get to start out careers as vice-presidents in daddy or mommy's companies. Putting depth of character before the depth of a bank account is a reflection or description of the mean-hearted capitalistic spirit, as the rich generally get that way on the backs of the poor who are the real seeds of wealth in a system that does not reward those who toil in obscurity.

Lynton Viñas is a woman with incredible depth of character who has always firmly turned her back on the idea that "things" are more important than people. She is a guiding light in the darkness of an economic system that crushes 99% under the jack-booted economic tyranny of the 1%. She never bends before the winds of adversity, and despite her 5:2 inch height (157.5 centremetres), stands tall against the winds of misery that blow like a hurricane across the path of those trapped in slavery to a cruel economic system.

Although she has no overriding desire to obtain wealth, she does understand why there are those who think that all problems can be solved with money. In a society where greed rules, she understands the power of wealth. Those without means are just a drain on the system, according to the politicians of right-wing mayhem, who never see a poor person they respect, for they see poverty as a disease, not a condition caused by a world where all the good things flow to those at the top while the rest beg for a crumb from the table of plenty.

The poor are disposable cogs in the giant machinery of capitalism that grinds the workers up and disposes of them when they have outlived their usefulness to the corporation. While professing to love Jesus, these are the people who turn their backs on everything he proclaimed about the poor and the wealthy in homily after homily pleading for those who had wealth to reach out with compassion.

Although she has no religion, Lynton Viñas walks in the footprints of that carpenter from Galilee in the way she treats people. In this adventure, detailing the lust for wealth that destroys men's souls, she will also walk into a hornets' nest of evil that will tax her survival instincts.

Chapter 1

Real Freedom and Its Value

Suddenly the desert changes,
The raw glare softens and clings,
Till the aching escarpment ranges
Stand up like the thrones of Kings.

Alan Wopner brooded continually over his fate. His days were filled with morbid self-pity, as he worked half-heartedly for the International Chemical Corporation. He missed the high life of Paris, and as the days passed he came to centre his resentment upon the security manager in the Lower Karoo Escarpment area near the little town of Matjiesfontein. He seethed with hatred for the authority of this man, his captain and immediate superior. This was a cold, taciturn man, inspiring little love in those directly beneath him, yet respected and feared by the modern day blacks who toiled mercilessly under his command.

Wopner was, like his boss, white, and accustomed to sitting for hours at a time glaring at his superior as the two lounged upon the veranda of their common quarters, smoking their evening cigars in a silence which neither seemed desirous of breaking. His senseless hatred of Wopner grew at last into a form of pure mania.

The superior's natural taciturnity was distorted into a studied attempt to insult Wopner because of his perceived shortcomings. Wopner imagined that his superior held him in contempt, and so he fumed inwardly until one evening his madness became suddenly homicidal. He fingered the butt of the revolver at his hip, his eyes narrowed and his brows contracted. At last he spoke.

"You have insulted me for the last time!" he cried, springing to his feet like a jack-rabbit in a cabbage patch. "I am tired of it, and I shall put up with it no longer without an accounting from you, you pig."

"The superior, an expression of surprise upon his features, turned toward Wopner. He had seen men before with the escarpment madness upon them, the madness of solitude and unrestrained brooding, and perhaps even touches of desert fever.

He rose and extended his hand to lay it upon the other's shoulder, as a sign of peace between the two. Quiet words of counsel were upon his lips; but they were never spoken. Wopner construed his superior's actions disdainfully. His revolver was on a level with the man's heart, and the latter had taken but a step when Wopner pulled the trigger. Without a moan, the man sank to the rough planking of the veranda, and as he fell the mists that had clouded Wopner's brain lifted, so that he saw himself and the deed that he had done in the same light that those who must judge him would see it.

He heard excited exclamations and wild rumblings of confusion from the quarters of the guards who protected the uranium deposits that were being mined, and he heard men running in his direction. They would seize him, and if they didn't kill him they would take him to the authorities where a properly ordered tribunal would do so just as effectively with a long, death-like prison sentence. It was those thoughts that motivated his urgent flight.

Wopner had no desire to die. Never before had he so yearned for life as in this moment. The men were nearing him. What was he to do? He glanced about as though searching for the tangible form of a legitimate excuse for his crime; but he could find only the body of the man he had so causelessly shot down.

In despair and mortal fear for his life, he turned rapidly and fled in great haste. Across the compound he ran, his revolver still clutched tightly in his hand. At the gates, a sentry halted him. Wopner did not pause to parley. He merely raised his weapon and shot down the innocent black man with great disdain, simply because of his colour. A moment later the fugitive had torn open the gates and vanished into the blackness of the Great Karoo, but not before he had transferred the rifle and ammunition belts of the dead sentry to his own person with incredible haste and determination.

All that night, Wopner fled farther and farther into the heart of the wilderness. Now and again the voice of a wild animal brought him to a listening halt; but with cocked and ready rifle he pushed ahead again, more fearful of the human huntsmen in his rear than of the wild carnivores heard ahead.

Dawn came at last, but still the man plodded on. All sense of hunger and fatigue were lost in the terrors of contemplated capture. He could think only of escape. He dared not pause to rest or eat until there was no further danger from pursuit, and so he staggered on until at last he fell and could rise no more. How long he had fled he did not know, or try to know. When he could flee no longer, the knowledge that he had reached his limit was hidden from him in the unconsciousness of utter exhaustion.

Thus it was that Ahmed Zam, Muslim Karoo night wanderer, found him. Ahmed's followers were for running a knife through the body of someone in a guard's uniform, indicating he was serving the oppressors who exploited the minerals of the Karoo; but Ahmed would have it otherwise. He would question the man. It was easier to question a man first and kill him afterward, than kill him first and then question him, he thought with a smile piercing his lips.

So he had Wopner carried to his nearby tent, and there his wives administered water and food in small quantities until at last he regained consciousness. As he opened his eyes, he saw the faces of strange people about him, and just outside the tent the figure of a man in a flowing white robe-like garment. Nowhere nearby were his pursuers from the mighty Chemical International Corporation to be seen.

Ahmed, in his flowing long white robe, turned with determination and seeing the open eyes of the prisoner, entered the tent. "I am Ahmed Zam," he announced. "Who are you, and from what are you fleeing?"

Wopner's eyes went wide, and his heart sank. He was in the clutches of the most notorious of cut-throats, the remnants of a mighty warrior clan of Muslims who had for years roamed the Karoo and hated all who dared enter their domain, even going so far as to engage in fire-fights with the modern South African constabulary who dared try and control their ancient ways. For years, the military forces had waged a fruitless war upon this man and his followers to no avail.

But in the very hatred of the man for outsiders, Wopner saw a faint ray of hope for himself. He, too, was an outcast and an outlaw. So far, at least, they possessed a common interest, and Wopner decided to play upon it for all that it might yield.

"I have heard of you," he very earnestly replied, "and was actually vehemently searching for you. My people have turned against me. I hate them. Even now their rent-a-cops are searching for me, to kill me. I knew that you would protect me from them, for you, too, hate the establishment as I do. In return, I will take service with you. I am a trained fighter. I will join your crusade against the evil of those who only seek to defame this great land."

Ahmed eyed him in silence. In his mind he revolved many thoughts, chief among which was that the unbeliever was lying. Of course there was the chance that he was not, and if he told the truth then his proposition was one well worthy of consideration, since fighting men were never overly plentiful in the wild Karoo, especially white men with the training and knowledge of military matters. He knew of the white guards at the Chemco compound from which it was easily deduced this man came as a result of the Chemco patch on his shirt shoulder. Ahmed was an incredibly astute observer and let nothing escape his keen eye.

Ahmed scowled and Wopner felt fear; but Wopner did not know Ahmed Zam, who was quite apt to scowl where another would smile, and smile where another would scowl.

"And if you have lied to me," said Ahmed, "I will cut out your heart while you are alive. What return, other than your life, do you expect for your services?"

"My keep only, at first," replied Wopner. "Later, if I am worth more, we can easily reach an understanding."

Wopner's only desire, at the moment, was to preserve his life. And so the agreement was reached and John Alan Wopner became a member of the motley crew that made a living by robbing and stealing all throughout the western Karoo.

For months the renegade Frenchman rode with the miscreants of discontent robbing and stealing from those who journeyed through the Karoo, his viciousness and cruelty far exceeding that of his fellow desperadoes. Ahmed Zam watched his recruit with eagle eye, and with a growing satisfaction, which finally found expression in a greater confidence in the man, and resulted in an increased independence of action for Wopner.

Finally, Ahmed took the Frenchman into his confidence to a great extent, and at last unfolded to him a pet scheme which the conniving Ahmed had long fostered, but which he never had found an opportunity to effect. With the aid of a European, however, the thing might be easily accomplished. He sounded out Wopner.

"You have heard of a man called Barbizon?" he asked.

Wopner nodded. "I have heard of him; but I do not know him. He is called by many the Lord of the Karoo."

"He is the lord of nothing. He is but a thorn in our side, worse than the government that is too far away to stymie our thievery. Anyway, the government doesn't care about the people out here, but Barbizon, on the other hand, thinks he is the Karoo people's protector. He and his high and mighty ideals interfere with the natural flow of the superiority of the mighty over the weak. He spoiled our plans about a year ago, when he and some little Filipino bitch came along and managed to stop us from exporting a few stolen atomic bombs built in the 1980's to some clients who were going to use them against the Americans."

"Yes," replied Wopner, "I have heard of her, too. She is beautiful, wise and cunning, but is she not in Cape Town, far from here?"

"I have word she is here in the Karoo again, visiting Barbizon. Now would be the opportune time to strike and get rid of two menaces at the same time."

"I hear Barbizon is heir to an estate in England, but he gave most of it away."

"Yes and therein lays the rub. You see, we can not only eliminate him, but make him pay handsomely with what he has left for causing us so much trouble," offered Ahmed.

"How my friend will he be forced to pay?"

"He recently, after he and the Filipino spoiled our plan to sell the atomic bombs that had been hidden away, after all believed the South African government had destroyed them, married a woman. Now, unlike me and my cohorts, who know women are nothing but chattel, he adores his wife and would do anything to prevent her harm. There are those in this world who are smart enough to know the value of a woman in gold, not love. She would bring a great price farther north, if we found it too difficult to collect ransom money from Barbizon. I trade with Arabs from Saudi regularly who willingly pay a big price for handsome women, and Barbizon's wife is beautiful. Ah, and then there is the fact the we know Lynton Viñas, known as the dynamic dynamo, who is also beautiful, is in Barbizon's camp now, visiting while her husband is away in Canada. These two women would bring much gold into our coffers."

Wopner bent his head in thought. What good remained in Wopner revolted at the thought of selling a woman into the slavery and degradation of a modern day harem in a nation that had refined the art of degradation for women, but went unpunished, because it sat on an ocean of oil. He looked up at Ahmed. He saw his eyes narrow, and he sensed he had recognized Wopner's antagonism to the plan. What would it mean if he refused? His life lay in the hands of this semi-barbarian, who esteemed the life of an unbeliever less highly than that of a dog. Wopner loved life. What were these women to him, anyway?

"You hesitate," murmured Ahmed as he stared directly into Wopner's eyes.

Wopner sighed. "I was but weighing the chances of success," he lied, "and my reward as a loyal confederate and white man would be invaluable as I can gain admittance to their home and table. You have no other with you who could do so much. The risk will be great. I should be well paid."

A smile crept across Ahmed's lips. "Well," he said as he tapped him on the shoulder, "yes, you shall be well paid. Now let us sit together and plan how best the thing may be done."

The two men squatted upon a soft rug beneath the fancy silks of Ahmed's opulent tent, for even in the wilds, those at the top of the economic ladder must have splendour while their lackey's languish in squalor. That is the way in the city and in the wilds. There is never any justice for those at the bottom.

The following day Wopner spent in overhauling his uniform, removing from it every vestige of evidence that might indicate its military-like purposes. From a heterogeneous collection of loot, Ahmed Zam procured a wide brimmed hat, and from his slave-like servants and followers, a party of porters, and tent boys to make up a modest safari for a photographic hunter of big game, even giving Wopner a huge hand-held video camera as proof he was a photographer in search of adventure. At the head of this party, Wopner set out from camp toward the escarpment area where the King of the Karoo, Barbizon, dwelled. In his heart was now beating with intensity a cause of nefarious intent.

Barbizon was immensely thrilled when Lynton Viñas, internationally acclaimed demon fighter, whose exploits had been made famous by her writer-husband before they were married, showed up at his escarpment home. Barbizon had been in love with Lynton, but her heart belonged to another. After the adventure chronicled in Wayne Frye's book, *Lynton's South African Adventure*, had been concluded, Lynton had returned to Cape Town, and Barbizon had met the beautiful Leila, married her and settled down in his tree house built among the Vachellia Shrub Trees on the mighty Karoo Escarpment.

As Lynton, Leila and Barbizon sat atop the tree house outlook, they could see, far in the distance, a safari making its way methodically and slowly toward Barbizon's home. There was always concern about intruders.

They sat quietly for a couple of hours, as the safari edged ever closer. Barbizon's incredibly keen eyes caught in the reflection of the sun the tall blond haired man riding on a grey horse at the head of the column. As they approached the tree house, the three went down to greet the safari. Wopner was playing his role in academy award fashion.

"I was completely lost," Wopner, now calling himself Alec Smith, was explaining. "My head man had never before been in this part of the country and the guides who were to have accompanied me from the last village we passed knew even less of the country than we. They finally deserted us two days since. I am very fortunate indeed to have stumbled so providentially upon your incredible abode. I do not know what I should have done had I not found you."

It was decided that Smith and his party should remain and rest, after which, Barbizon would provide them detailed directions to lead them safely into the wilds where Smith could capture the images he so vehemently desired.

In his guise of a French gentleman of leisure and wealth, Wopner found little difficulty in deceiving his hosts and in ingratiating himself with all three of them; but the longer he remained the less hopeful he became of an easy accomplishment of his designs.

It seemed the two women never were alone at any great distance from the tree house, and the intense savage loyalty of those in the compound to Barbizon and the two women seemed to absolutely preclude the possibility of a successful attempt at a contrived forcible abduction, or of the bribery of any of the workers there. He sent a runner back to Ahmed to tell him to march on the compound, as he needed more manpower to capture the women.

Two long, arduous days passed, and Wopner was no nearer the fulfillment of his plan in so far as he could judge, than upon the day of his arrival, but at that very moment something occurred which gave him renewed hope and set his mind upon an even greater reward than the women's ransom.

There was no internet in this wild area, and a runner had arrived at the tree house with the mail. Barbizon had spent the afternoon in his study reading and contemplating on something. At dinner he seemed distraught, and early in the evening he excused himself and retired, with Leila and Lynton following him very soon after. Wopner, sitting upon the veranda, could hear the voices of Leila and Barbizon in earnest discussion, and having realized that something unusual was afoot, he quietly rose from his chair, and keeping well in the shadows of the home made his silent way to a point beneath the window of the room in which his host and hostess slept. Here he listened, and not without result, for almost the first words he overheard filled him with excitement.

"There is," said Barbizon, "reason to think that if I do not go to recover some of the jewels, the tribe will lose to the government their entire village, as they have not the money to fight against the land grab of another corporation that has bought government influence. Lawyers are expensive, but I must aid these people who have no use for the minerals this company wants to dig from the ground underneath the village. The modern world is ruled by greed, and all these people want is to be left alone in the place they think is paradise. I must go to where Sheik of the Karoo, Omar Bin Abi, hid the great treasure that I promised to use if the people he loved ever needed it. This is the time. I cannot let our friends suffer the fate of so many others who have been displaced from their ancestral homes by the greed that now has imprisoned the entire world to the 1% who simply can never have enough. I shall not sit idly by without helping those who cry for a hand up."

"Oh, my dear Barbizon," cried a concerned Leila, and Wopner could feel the shudder through her voice as he leaned in closer to the window, "is there no other way? I cannot bear to think of you returning to that awful place where the jewels are."

"Barbizon said almost jokingly, "Maybe I should take the dynamic dynamo with me. She came here saying she wanted a little adventure while she was off from school. I would let you come along too, just to the outskirts of the Valley of Quanzi."

As Leila was about to reply, a knock on the door made them perk up, and a soft voice said, "May I come in please?"

It was Lynton, and Leila replied, "Yes."

Lynton stood there in the doorway as she said, "I could not help but notice your consternation this evening Barbizon. I do not want to interfere, but I am your and Leila's friend. Is there something I can do to help?"

As Wopner continued to listen, they explained to Lynton the problems the nearby tribe was having with the government wanting to confiscate their land, remove them to another area, and allow a mining corporation to destroy their way of life for profit. When Barbizon said he knew of a place where there were magnificent jewels just waiting to be snatched, so that the Arori Tribe could fight the encroachment in court, Lynton, after listening intently, offered a homily of discontent. "It makes no difference where in the world you are, it is impossible to escape the culture of greed that spreads like a plague across the planet. My dear Wayne has fought against the corporations and the privileged classes all his life, and you know I am no stranger to the conflict between good and evil. I would be privileged to go with you if I may. I may be small, but I have the drive, desire and determination to stand against any tyranny promulgated against the weak and defenceless. How about it?"

Leila smiled as she said, "I just told him to take you along. Harvest time is near, and I need to stay here and see that our grapes come in on time, because the winery is all we have to support ourselves and the 20 people who call this compound home." She then turned to Barbizon and said with great seriousness, "Come take her along. Then I know she'll keep a close eye on you and make sure you stay out of trouble."

Looking at Lynton, Barbizon said, "The inhabitants of Quanzi will never know that we have been there if we are careful. There should be no danger at all if you want to come, Lynton."

Lynton, smiling broadly now, said, "Darn it, a little trouble is so much fun. I mean my middle name is *Danger*!"

Wopner remained, listening intently, for a short time, and then, extremely confident that he had overheard all that was necessary, and fearing discovery, returned to the giant porch alongside the inner house, where he sat in a lounge chair as Lynton walked up and said, "Having trouble sleeping?"

"I am. In fact I think I shall sleep here in this lovely spot."

Lynton's brown body's gorgeous curves showing through the white robe as the moon's light filtered through it, said, "Good idea."

She walked away nonchalantly as Wopner gazed at her, thinking the thoughts so many men cannot control. He sighed and drifted off to sleep, dreaming of riches and Lynton.

The following morning, an aroused Wopner announced his intention of making an early departure, and asked Barbizon's permission to take some wildlife photos below the Karoo Escarpment, which he heartedly granted. He bade all goodbye and sat out toward the towering escarpment, while sending another runner to tell Ahmed he was on the trail of even greater treasure, and that Ahmed should raid the home of Barbizon, as he was leading him away to make it easier to capture his wife.

As Wopner made his way toward the escarpment, he eyed Barbizon and Lynton leaving through binoculars. With six porters and fourteen other miscreants in tow, they hid below the escarpment, waiting to march after Barbizon and the little imp of a women with him to discover where the treasure was hidden, as visions of riches danced in his head.

So, it was on the path taken by Barbizon, stripped to the loin cloth and armed after the primitive fashion he best loved (only a knife), that Wopner moved cautiously in pursuit toward the place where he assumed great riches lay. Wopner, skilled as a trail-follower, stayed a good 10 kilometres back through the long, hot day.

While Wopner trailed Barbizon, now discarding his Range Rover, Ahmed rode on his trusty steed like a bold raider of olden days with his entire following southward toward Barbizon's farm, and the tantalizing female morsel that awaited capture.

Meanwhile, to Barbizon and Lynton, their expedition was in the nature of a holiday outing. To them both, civilization was at best but an outward veneer. Lynton, now feeling the intensity of the desert heat, tore the bottoms of her pants exposing her shapely legs. They were extremely long for such a short woman. The calves were a work of art, flexing perfectly from the years she spent as a dancer. Each stride also emphasized tense, taunt thighs that made even Barbizon look intently at what was an extraordinarily beautiful woman with a body that seemed to have been sculpted by Michelangelo. Her stomach, with a slight protrusion, was exposed as she knotted her shirt right above her navel. Her breasts seemed to be fighting for freedom from the tight fitting blouse that contained what she called Mount James and Mount Wayne in honour of her beloved husband. The blouse hung off her shoulders that were prominent from her thinness, and above those was that soft, cute little dimpled throat, which in turn, seemed to glide ever so gently to an absolutely perfect chin below the most succulent thick lips imaginable, lips puckered with a rosy red slightly licked look that appeared to be begging for a kiss. Her flat Asian nose was perfectly formed in exotic proportion. The dark, almost black eyes, twinkled with a hint of mischievousness. Her dark brown hair cascaded down her back coming far below the waist, and it fluttered gently about the most perfectly shaped butt that wiggled and jiggled like a freshly dished out bowl of Jell-O.

She was not unaware of the effect she had on men, but she never looked upon herself as sexy. She felt she was just a simple woman in a world where she cared not what people thought of her looks, but was far more concerned about what people thought of her character. She exuded a nomenclature of such unconcern about her looks that it actually made her more immensely appealing in a sublime way, as she did not flaunt her sexiness. She was a woman of immense charisma, which was, without a doubt, her greatest asset. She was a woman who knew she was beautiful but was not arrogant about it, as she knew that outer beauty faded with age, but that inner beauty lasted a life-time.

Lynton had no shame, which made her an unassailable individual who never embraced judgemental arrogance. She hated the unmitigated shams and the hypocrisies of so-called civilization and with the clear vision of an unspoiled mind she had penetrated to the rotten core of the heart of the modern world of greed, the cowardly greed for ease and the safe-guarding of property rights. She loved art, music and literature, but saw it being demeaned and dumbed down by those who tried to homogenize everything, because it made it easier to impose uniformity that is needed to control people, and make them acquiescent to bowing before the privileged class that rule with almost total impunity.

For her, there was a grand freedom in the wilds of the Karoo, in the battle for survival, amid hunger and death and danger, in the face of a magnificence manifested in the display of nature's forces, where there is born all that is finest and best in the human heart and mind. There was a simplicity here one could not find in the city.

Marvel at how nature could ever find space
For many strange contrasts in one human face:
There's thought and no thought,
And there's paleness and bloom,
And bustle and sluggishness, pleasure and gloom.

There's weakness, strength redundant and vain;
Such strength as, if ever affliction and pain
Could pierce through with softness to please
Would be rational peace, a philosopher's ease.

It matters not when one fails or succeeds,

Attention is given to all about and their needs;
Pride with no envy, there's so much of joy;
And mildness, and spirit both forward and coy.

There's freedom, and sometimes a diffident stare,
Shame scarcely seeming to know that she's there.
There's virtue, the title it surely may claim,
For heaven here be worthy of the name.

This picture from nature may seem to depart,
But peace here runs away with your heart.
Be not put aside for here love does abide.
This is where Lynton finds her passion,
And embraces it in exuberate fashion.

So, Lynton was called to nature in the spirit of a lover keeping a long deferred tryst after a period behind prison walls. Her prison had always been the city, where freedom seemed homogenized and bastardized. She would have been at home in the Garden of Eden, frolicking about naked with no shame. This was a woman who embraced freedom and understood that most people who thought they were free had simply swallowed the propaganda fed by those in control. She saw through the veneer of the modern world that had been turned over to corporations that had truly convinced people happiness can be bought for that proverbial 20 pieces of silver for which people sold their souls. This was a woman who knew real freedom, and she understood its value.

Chapter 2

Die in the Agony He Deserves

Ramparts of past slaughter and peril,
Blazing, amazing ,shining and aglow
'Twixt the sky-line's belting beryl
And the wine-dark flats below.

Royal the pageant closes
Lit by the last of the sun.
Opal and ash-of-roses,
As the long day is done.

Lynton and Barbizon lay awake in the middle of a clearing, as a fire blazed boldly while their ten accompanying men were in a circle, backs to the fire, sleeping with rifles in hand in case an animal dare enter among them. A single guard walked a circle in the camp as yellow eyes out of the darkness beyond the camp peered at those lying there. The moans and coughing of the roaming animals mingled with the myriad noises of the lesser denizens of the Karoo to fan the savage flame in the breast of Barbizon, who was always at home in the wild, and Lynton saw how he loved it there, and she loved it, too. Barbizon tossed upon his bed of grass, sleepless, for an hour and then he rose, noiseless and stealthy as a stalking panther. He looked down at dear Lynton, smiled, then to the surprise of none there who saw him arise, he bounded into the darkness. With his flaming eyes, he climbed a great tree and curled up in peace.

The moon shone full upon him and Lynton looked up at a man she had grown to admire. She had spurned his romantic advances, but that did not mean she did not find him an extraordinary man. Her Wayne had lived in cities most of his life, from New York City to Los Angeles, finally turning his back on the jungles of concrete and steel when he gave up hope on America ever changing and embracing compassion. He moved to Canada's Vancouver Island, finding refuge from the evils of a society where greed was aggrandized as an enviable trait, but even there the long tentacles of the American society of greed wrapped its maniacal tentacles around those who fell victim to the pursuit of material things rather than peace and harmony. There was no escaping the evil of crass unyielding consumerism and the ever growing, unrestrained power of the 1% who ruled the world like ancient, all-powerful feudal lords.

Yet, here in the Karoo was one mighty man who stood boldly against the evil of greed that had become so pervasive, but even he was driven to search for treasure in order to assist those who were being trampled by the jack-booted foot of capitalism, as the government served the interests of corporations before the interests of the people. So-called democracy had been hijacked by corporations and the wealthy, and it appeared all but a few hold-outs like Lynton and Barbizon stood in bold defiance against the sweeping tide of greed that had consumed the entire world with its unending search to obtain more and more for the fewer and fewer.

Far away, Wopner and his charges huddled in the darkness, shivering from the desert cold, but eschewing a fire for fear Barbizon might see the flames in the distance, and realize he was being trailed. Meanwhile, Barbizon looked into the night sky with thousands of twinkling stars and thought of how he loved his homeland.

Barbizon, the mighty, surveyed all he knew.
Far from his tree house home,
He grasp the meaning of the broad Karoo.
The bush and the wild flowers bloom,
And up rose he to a darkening view,
Strange stars twinkling of doom.

Barbizon's powers of observation were as keen as a stalking panther. He looked to the south, and knew there was something there, something in the darkness. Were they being followed? There was no smoke from a campfire, but there was the smell of men far behind them that his sensitive nostrils sniffed on the night breeze as he lay on a branch high in the tree. Should he curtail the mission, turn backward and confront whomever it was following? No, what they needed was critical to the survival of his friends, the Arori. He would worry about whoever was trailing them at a later date. Now was not the time.

Sloughed from him was the last vestige of artificial caste, as once again he was the primeval man, the first man, the highest physical caste type of the human race. His was a world valiant and glorified by its simplicity of purpose.

Down wind, as he sensed the elusive spoor of men in the far distance, he was unable to sleep, wondering what the pursuers wanted. With a sense of perception, transcending that of ordinary man as to be inconceivable to others, he could actually smell that his followers were made up of one white man and several blacks, along with maybe a few half-castes. It was troubling, but he saw no need to risk the lives of the 10 in his party, and, of course, dear Lynton, like his dear Leila, now a treasure of the Karoo.

In his right hand was the long hunting knife of his father and in his heart the pounding blood of concern for those down below. His peering eyes blazed into the direction from which the wind had borne the smell of his pursuers. A moment later the grasses at one side of the clearing about 100 metres away parted and a panther's eyes could be seen in the brush, as it obviously smelt the spores of those at the encampment. His yellow-green eyes were fastened suddenly upon Barbizon, as he halted just within the clearing and glared, seeing a tasty morsel there in the tree.

The panther stood waving its tail gently to and fro. Always, Barbizon watched him, guessing what was passing in the little brain of the carnivore and well it was that he did watch him, for the panther could stand it no longer. His tail shot suddenly erect, and Barbizon knew it was about to charge, leap up the tree with its razor like claws and attempt to make a midnight snack of him.

There was suddenly a staring contest between the two, and it was obvious to the panther that this man was his equal in the wilds. The animal was roaring and resentful; but in the very centre of the clearing his sounds were suddenly hushed and Barbizon saw the head lower and flatten out, the body crouch and the long tail quiver, as the beast slunk cautiously toward the trees upon the opposite side.

Immediately, Barbizon was alert. He lifted his head and sniffed the slow, jungle breeze. What was it that had attracted the panther's attention? Just as the panther disappeared among the trees beyond the clearing, Barbizon caught upon the down-coming wind the explanation of his new interest, the scent of man was wafted strongly to his sensitive nostrils. Barbizon lowered himself from the tree and cautiously moved through the scrub. The panther and Barbizon saw the animal's quarry almost simultaneously, though both had known before it came within the vision of their eyes that it was a small black man. Their sensitive nostrils had told them this much and Barbizon's keen scent indicated it was an older male, for race, sex and age each has its own distinctive scent. It was indeed an old man that made his way alone through the gloomy desert night, a wrinkled, dried up, little old man hideously scarred, tattooed and strangely garbed.

The panther charged the old man, slashing away with claws. At the same instant Barbizon leaped full upon the panther's back, plunging his knife into the tawny side behind the left shoulder. With a roar of pain and rage, the panther reared up and fell backward upon Barbizon; but still the mighty Lord of the Karoo clung to his hold and repeatedly the long knife plunged rapidly into the animal's side. Over and over the animal rolled, clawing and biting at the air, roaring and growling horribly in savage attempt to reach the thing upon its back.

More than once was Barbizon almost brushed from his hold. All the while, there was mass confusion in the encampment as all scurried up from slumber.

Finally, the constant piercing of the flesh with a knife subdued the mighty panther as it began to whine like a kitten, beaten into submission by Barbizon. It breathed its last just as those aroused from slumber lurched into the clearing, guns at the ready, but there was no need, for the mighty Barbizon had prevailed.

The old man lay, torn and bleeding, unable to drag himself away, had watched the terrific battle between the two. His sunken eyes glittered and his wrinkled lips moved over toothless gums as he mumbled weird incantations, probably to one of the many gods that men somehow think guide their lives. He gazed upon Barbizon, as Lynton and the others rushed to his side. The old black man's eyes went wider in amazement at this white man who had battled a panther with bare hands and knife, coming out triumphant. What wonderful sort of creature was this he thought? Gropingly backward into the past, he reached the tides of memory, until at last he seized upon a faint picture, faded and yellow with the passing years of a lithe, white-skinned man swaggering through the Karoo. The old eyes blinked and a great fear came into them, the superstitious fear of one who believes in ghosts, spirits and demons. This was religion that had a firm grip on so many who clung to the past in the great Karoo, when demons, goblins and a spirits danced about to the music of superstition.

As the band gathered about Barbizon to see that he was alright, Barbizon waved them off and turned his immediate attention to the man. He had slain the panther to save the old man, as the old and the young are the best targets of opportunity for predators in the wild and in the city. As he saw the old man lying helpless and dying before him, pity touched his heart. He stood by as Lynton stooped and tried to stem the flow of blood from the old man.

The old man shook convulsively and closed his eyes. When he opened them again, there was in them a resignation to whatever horrible fate awaited him in the hereafter as he said in English, "Why did you not just let it kill me?"

"We are all animals," replied Barbizon, "but you are of my species and for that reason I wanted to protect you."

For a moment the old man was silent. When he spoke it was evidently after some little effort to muster his courage. "I knew you of old," he said, "when you roamed the Karoo in the country of Mombata, the chief. I was his under chief, when you lived with the wild animals in a time when they roamed more freely and made life miserable in our village. You tamed the beasts there and they stopped attacking the village. Tell me before I die, are you man or devil?"

Barbizon laughed. "I am but a man."

The old fellow sighed and shook his head. "You have tried to save me from a devil inhabiting the panther then," he said. "For that I shall reward you. I am a great witch-doctor. Listen to me, white man! I see bad days ahead of you. It is writ in my own blood which I have smeared upon my palm, a god greater even than you will rise up and strike you down. Turn back! Turn back before it is too late. Danger lies ahead of you and danger lurks behind; but greater is the danger before. I see. I see…" He paused and drew a long, gasping breath. Then he crumpled into a little, wrinkled heap and died. Non-believers, Barbizon and Lynton, stared at one another, wondering what else the delusional dying man had seen in the throes of death.

Neither Barbizon nor Lynton were capable of sleep; although, after placing the old man's body high in a tree to keep it from wild animals, they tried. They both looked at one another, without words, thinking about the warning of the old witch-doctor before he embraced eternity, then drifted off to sleep. When they awoke, they did not turn back, for both were unafraid, though had they known what lay in store for Leila, they would have flown with great haste back to Barbizon's home and allowed the jewels of Omar Bin Abi to lie forever hidden in their forgotten storehouse.

Barbizon and Lynton forged steadily ahead toward their rendezvous with destiny foretold by a dying man; although they were unaffected by what they considered delusional ramblings. Behind them, like a vulture in pursuit of a carcass to ravage, slunk Wopner, evil intent within his heart.

At the edge of a desolate valley, overlooking a vast plain, lay the land called by the people of the Karoo *the place of evil*, for it was there that even the government dared not go, because within lived the remnants of the whites who had refused to accept the demise of the evil racial segregation system called apartheid. They had moved into this isolated valley away from a world where the blacks and coloureds of South African society had gained their freedom. They hated the new South Africa.

Wopner, leaving behind his party of men for fear of detection, had scaled the cliffs alone behind Lynton and Barbizon's party, and hidden through the day among the rough boulders of the mountain top. The boulder-strewn plain between the valley's edge and the mighty granite-like escarpment to the north gave him sufficient cover from detection, as he stared down at the lower escarpment.

Barbizon moved toward the place where the treasure was hidden, as told him by Omar Bin Abi so many years ago, when he befriended Barbizon and told him that if the people of the Arori tribe ever needed financial largesse it was awaiting them in a place where he was no longer welcome, but because of Barbizon's tenacious nature, he might be able to access unimaginable riches should the people ever need it. Barbizon had no doubts of Bin Abi's authenticity, because his love for the Arori was unimpeachable. Now, he stood gazing down at the place where wealth laid waiting.

Wopner, clawing fearfully during the perilous ascent, sweating in terror, almost palsied by fear, but spurred on by avarice, followed upward, until at last he stood upon the summit of the rocky hill, where he looked down at the place he had only heard of from those who either embraced its brazen racism or hated it with a passion. This was the place where the evil past of South Africa had come, not to die, but to be embraced with vigour. Like the visages of racism in America that still festered among far too many in the southern USA, and were promoted by a demagogue in the White House who effectively appealed to people's hatred, here, in this peaceful looking valley the evil of the past was glorified and taught to the children who were being brainwashed to accept the idea of racial superiority. Like placing hand-over-heart to pledge allegiance to a flag and invoke God's blessing for tyranny or standing dutiful for a national anthem that glorified violence, this was a place that promoted devotion to a lie. There was palatable evil in that valley, an evil that is as old as mankind itself – the arrogant evil of belief in one man's superiority over another. This was a barren place, barren of acceptance and filled with hatred.

Barbizon and Lynton were nowhere in sight. For a time Wopner hid behind one of the lesser boulders that were scattered over the top of the hill, but, seeing or hearing nothing of the party he was trailing, he crept from his place of concealment to undertake a systematic search of his surroundings, in the hope that he might discover the location of the treasure in ample time to make his escape, for it was now the Frenchman's desire merely to locate the treasure, allow Barbizon to take what he needed, as he was not greedy like the Frenchman, then after Barbizon had departed, he might come in safety with his followers and carry away as much as he could transport.

He found the narrow cleft leading downward into the heart of the valley along well-worn, granite steps. He advanced ever so cautiously to the dark mouth of a tunnel into which the path disappeared; but here he halted, fearing to enter, lest he meet Barbizon returning from the other side.

Barbizon and Lynton, leaving their comrades behind to avoid detection with a large group that might stir up dust, were far ahead of Wopner now, having worked their way through a long tunnel-like cavern. Although Barbizon was but 19 when Bin Abi shared the secret of the treasure, his furtive mind recalled every detail of where it was hidden. They groped their way along the rocky passage and soon came to a huge bolder marked with the sign of the cross, which was certainly strange since Bin Abi was a Muslim. Perhaps it was his own little private joke, because Barbizon knew him as a man who, although an observant Muslim, respected people of all religions, and even those with no religion. The top of the cross pointed the way to a large boulder that hung precariously on the edge of the small escarpment hillside. Barbizon took Lynton by the hand as he edged his way onward to the front of the boulder. As they reached the front of the boulder, clinging to a small ledge, Barbizon put his foot under a small portion of the lower part of the boulder and felt a stone like peddle. He pushed hard on it, and a creaking noise could be heard to the right of the boulder, as part of the hillside seemed to open up. There was a small opening through which the two of them crawled. A moment later they stood within the treasure chamber, where, ages since, long-dead hands had arranged the lofty rows of precious ingots for the rulers of that great continent which now lies submerged beneath the waters of the Atlantic to the west of the Karoo. This was treasure from the lost continent of

Atlantis placed there thousands of years ago by people intent on protecting treasure from a sinking continent that become the subject of legends for all time.

No sound broke the stillness of the subterranean vault. There was no evidence that another had discovered the forgotten wealth since last time Omar Bin Abi had visited it so many years ago. There was a dark foreboding atmosphere there.

By this time, Wopner had worked his way alongside the tunnel and over the top of it to be within 100 metres of the boulder under which Lynton and Barbizon had disappeared. Hidden from view, he watched as they emerged with nothing in their arms. Why? Wopner, from the concealment of a jutting huge boulder, watched them pass up from the shadows of boulder below and advance toward the edge of the hill and disappear into the tunnel. Then Wopner, slipping stealthily from his hiding place, made his way to the boulder and found the rock peddle, pushed on it and dropped into the sombre darkness of the entrance and disappeared.

Barbizon and Lynton made their way through the tunnel again, and when they emerged on the other side, Barbizon raised his voice in imitating the thunderous roar of a jackal. Thrice, at regular intervals, he repeated the call, standing in attentive silence for several minutes after the echoes of the third call had died away. And then, from far across the valley, faintly, came an answering roar. One of his men had heard the signal and replied, so now they could approach at sundown and help carry out the loot.

In the treasure vault, Wopner hid in the far reaches where darkness kept him from view, while Barbizon and Lynton returned, waiting for the arrival of the others. The chamber was dark, but still the sparkle of the jewels provided a twinkling type light. It was as if all the riches of the world were there in that chamber. This was such wealth that it dwarfed anything man could image.

As they waited, a subdued Barbizon said they would carry as much as possible from the chamber and have it waiting, not telling anyone just how much treasure there was for fear some might be tempted if they saw the immense wealth that lay in the chamber.

Six trips were made in the five hours before the men reached the two, and at the end of that time Lynton and Barbizon had transported forty-eight gold ingots to the edge of the great boulder, carrying upon each trip a load that would dwarf the South African budget for a year.

As they removed treasure, Wopner cowered in the shadows at the far end of the long chamber, his mouth salivating with glee at what he had discovered. He was the richest man in the world!

As they left the chamber, Barbizon turned back for a glimpse of the fabulous wealth upon which they had ensconced all that was needed in order to help people in the fight against greed, thinking that to defeat greed he had turned to greed.

Behind them, the spy waited patiently, and then as Barbizon stepped out from the chamber, he hollered back into the darkness, "The chamber can only be opened and closed from the outside. So rest in peace with the treasure you covet Mr. Smith or whatever your name is."

As Barbizon stepped on the stone pebble, Lynton looked at him with surprise while the ten who had accompanied them began picking up the bags loaded with treasure. Barbizon, smiling, said, "Yes, he has been trailing us all along. I smelled his spores, smelled the residue of the cigar he smoked back at my home."

Lynton, although bothered by what Barbizon had done, knew better than to question him, because his justice was like that of the beasts of the Karoo, swift and final.

Barbizon said, "Come now; let the greedy miscreant die in the agony he deserves."

Chapter 3

As Plain as the Printed Page of an Open Book

The twilight swallows the thicket,
The starlight reveals the ridge.
The Karoo shrills to the picket.
The treasure is hope's bridge.

Few they were in the land so lonely,
Where the bright jewels did shine.
They were there to help only
With treasure from the Atlantis mine.

In the darkness Wopner rose and stretched his cramped muscles as fear overwhelmed him. He stretched forth a hand and caressed a golden ingot near him, thinking that he would die rich. He raised the ingot from its immemorial resting place and weighed it in his hands. He clutched it to his bosom in an ecstasy of avarice, but realized he was trapped. He wandered to the opening that was now covered by the giant boulder that had closed with the touch of Barbizon's death foot.

Meanwhile, Barbizon dreamed of the happy homecoming which lay before him, of dear arms about his neck, and a soft cheek pressed to his; but there rose to dispel that dream the memory of the old man and his dire warning as he lay dying. And then, in the span of a few brief seconds, the hopes of both these men were shattered. The one forgot even his greed in the panic of terror as he screamed in the darkness for help. The other was plunged into total forgetfulness of the past by a jagged fragment of rock that came flying down from above, which gashed a deep cut upon his head.

One instant all was quiet, the next the world rocked, the tortured sides of the narrow passageway along which they were making their way, split and crumbled, great blocks of granite, dislodged from above, tumbled into the narrow way, choking it, and the walls bent inward upon the wreckage. Beneath the blow of a fragment of the rock, Barbizon, covering Lynton with his body to prevent her injury, staggered back against the hillside, tumbling downward while the rest of the party carrying treasure was hurled over the side, plunging to their deaths.

Lynton knew instantly that what had occurred was an earthquake. She lay on the side of the escarpment, surprised that she and Barbizon had tumbled all the way down to where the opening into the chamber was. The mountainside was still rumbling, and fearful that they might tumble off the side, she thought only of the safety that might be offered by the chamber, so she put her foot under the boulder and opened up the chamber.

Wopner, thrilled by the slow opening of the outward door, staggered to his feet when he found himself unhurt. Groping his way toward the far end of the chamber, he breathed a nervous sigh of relief, for the impenetrable gloom had accentuated the terrors of his situation. Lynton pulled Barbizon into the chamber and stood staring at the shocked Wopner.

Barbizon was unconscious now, but still Wopner drew back in sudden fear of detection; but a second glance convinced him that Barbizon was dead. From a great gash in the man's head, a pool of blood had collected upon the floor. Ignoring Lynton, he bolted for the passageway and safety, but his renewed hopes were soon dashed. Just beyond the doorway he found the passage completely clogged and choked by impenetrable masses of shattered falling rock. Once more he turned and re-entered the treasure chamber. He ignored Lynton as if she did not exist.

Suddenly, he saw some light in the far reaches of the chamber. Had another entrance been exposed by the earthquake? He moved toward the light and there was another opening where there was a narrow passageway. As Lynton cradled Barbizon in her arms, she watched helplessly as Wopner made his way out, ascending a flight of stone steps to another corridor twenty feet above the level of the first. The flickering sun light led to a yawning pit, apparently terminating at the tunnel he was traversing.

Before him was a circular shaft. Below him, at a great distance, he saw the light reflected back from the surface of a pool of water. He had come upon a well. He peered across the black void, and there, upon the opposite side, he saw the continuation of the tunnel; but how was he to span the gulf?

He gathered himself for the leap across the chasm. Going back twenty paces, he took a running start, and at the edge of the well, leaped upward and outward in an attempt to gain the opposite side. In utter darkness he flew through space, clutching outward for a hold should his feet miss the invisible ledge. He made it.

He moved steadily forward for what seemed an eternity but was only half an hour, and he began to feel as though a great weight had been lifted from his shoulders. He took a step toward what appeared to be a large open area, and then he halted, wide-eyed in astonishment and terror, as a horde of frightful men rushed in upon him.

They were the white people from the village below, who were apparently in the middle of some ceremony. They were dressed in black robes that had a giant devil like creature embossed on the front. It had two ram like horns emanating from the head, huge arched brows, horrendous carnivore teeth, claws for hands and hoofs for feet. With a scream, he turned to flee back into the lesser terrors from whence he had come. They blocked the way; they seized him, and though he fell, grovelling upon his knees before them, begging for his life, they bound him and hurled him to the floor and dragged him forward.

A beautiful woman, obviously some type of priestess, naked from the waist up, came into the circular chamber where he lay as he was raised up and placed upon a bloody altar where cold sweat dripped from his every pore as the priestess raised a curved, sacrificial knife above him. The death chant fell upon his tortured ears. His staring eyes wandered to the golden goblets on another altar behind the priestess, knowing that it would be his blood they would be drinking from those goblets.

Suddenly there was a loud roar that vibrated through the chamber. The priestess lowered her dagger. Her eyes went wide in horror as she screamed and fled madly toward the exit. The others followed her in terrible fright. Wopner strained his neck to catch a sight of the cause of their panic, and when, at last he saw it, he too went cold in dread, for what his eyes beheld was the figure of a huge panther, at least five feet high with massive legs and snarling teeth, methodically making its way toward the altar. He shivered with fear.

While all this was transpiring, Ahmed Zam, was leading his band of soon-to-be raiders toward Barbizon's compound. They had left all vehicles behind and were now on horses, as they closed in on the tree house that Barbizon called home.

Leila was tending the vineyard with the head man, Mamgabi, when they noticed some dust rising in the distance. They ran to the tree house, where Leila got out her binoculars and observed what she knew instantly was a hostile band of raiders. There was a cell-phone there, but it was a futile effort in a dead zone when she tried to contact the authorities. They had weapons, but since there were only twenty and the band heading their way was maybe 30, Leila insisted that they would simply give the band whatever they wanted and hope for the best.

Leila urged Mamgabi to go and find Barbizon to let him know what was happening. He refused, but she kept insisting that he was more fleet afoot than she was, and that they would not kill a woman, because it was no doubt the dreaded Ahmed Zam, who took women for slaves to be bartered to the harems of those who still lived lives of debauchery in nations where women were nothing more than property to be bought and sold.

Grudgingly, Mamgabi tried to slip away into the vast Karoo, as Ahmed approached Leila's home. He came upon Ahmed and met instant death from the hot lead spit by Ahmed's automatic weapon. "Fire not upon the woman!" cried Ahmed. "Who harms her, dies."

Leila stood bravely on the veranda, firing her rifle down at the men making their way up the rope stairs, but alas, they were simply too many. She was surrounded and disarmed. Without a word they dragged her from the lofty perch, and she did not fight them any longer, for it was fruitless.

She saw her home plundered of all that represented intrinsic worth in the eyes of the raiders, and then she saw the torch applied, and the flames lick up what remained. Horses were now brought up, as she pleaded for them not to kill her dear workers, but they were mercilessly slaughtered with knifes across their necks, all but the beautiful young women, who were tied into a chain rope with her and led away for a fate they could not comprehend.

Meanwhile, Lynton had found some dripping water in a nearby wall and was bringing Barbizon back to consciousness. Slowly he rose to a sitting posture, signalling with his eyes that he was OK. They looked about, and Lynton pointed toward the area where Wopner had disappeared into darkness.

They meandered forward, finally reaching the well. Barbizon went back to the chamber and found a rope. He told Lynton to stay above while he lowered himself to see what was below. He tied off the rope on a nearby boulder and descended into the well, reaching the water, where he dived in. There was light filtering into the well from the right side where a small opening occurred in the wall. He swam to it, and drew himself out upon the wet floor of a tunnel. He called up to Lynton and told her to lower herself down. Together, they crawled a long distance in what appeared to be a straight passage. The floor was slippery, as though at times the rising waters of the well overflowed and flooded it.

An exclamation of delight broke from their lips at the sight of a large chamber where on a giant series of stone tables lay magnificent jewels. There were huge chests scattered all about, and within them were more precious jewels. Unwittingly, they had stumbled upon the forgotten jewel-room of more contents from the people of Atlantis, a room that Omar Bin Abi had probably not known about.

Suddenly, they heard a mighty roar to their left. They moved to an opening and peered in to see a huge panther, larger than Barbizon had ever seen, slowly moving toward a tied up man on an altar. Just as the panther approached the altar, Lynton stumbled and made a noise. It turned and stared at the two.

It was then that, to the panther's surprise, Barbizon charged it, screaming at the top his lungs, knife in hand. In shock, the panther turned and bounded out an opening nearby that glistened with the filtering light of the sun.

Wopner was astounded as Barbizon was eyeing him, Lynton standing meekly by his side. Barbizon told Lynton, "Untie him. I was wrong to leave him in that place. We'll take him back, so he can face justice."

Wopner knew that he had no immediate chance of escape, but he still had designs on the jewels, and when Barbizon said, "we shall go back to the chamber we crawled from, take as many jewels as we can and turn them over to the Arori," Wopner knew he could use these two to help him carry the jewels that he would eventually steal.

As the three, laden down with the jewels, made their way back toward Barbizon's home, they came upon the remnants of Wopner's party of men, all with their throats slit and terribly mutilated, obviously done by the white villagers.

Wopner coveted the jewels and vowed to himself that what was here with the three would never be shared with Ahmed, as he would dispatch these two eventually and take the jewels.

The journey was long and arduous, until they finally came over the hills of the Wasuri Plain. Beyond, grazing herds of elk dotted the level landscape, while closer to the river a bull buffalo, his head and shoulders protruding from the reeds watched the advancing three for a moment, only to turn at last and disappear into the safety of his dank and gloomy retreat. Barbizon had bound Wopner, and kept a close eye on him, always making him lead the way.

Barbizon looked out across the familiar vista with a tinge of excitement as he thought of Leila waiting for him. Trepidation sat in as Barbizon and Lynton could not believe their eyes, there was no tree-home, no barns, no out-houses. What was the explanation for the obvious havoc that had been wrought in what was a valley of peace? Slowly, there filtered into Wopner's consciousness an explanation of the havoc that had been wrought since last his eyes had rested upon it. As planned, Ahmed Zam had been there and captured Leila.

When, at last they crossed the trampled garden and stood before the charred ruins of the tree house, the greatest fears became convictions in light of the evidence about them.

Remnants of human dead, half devoured by prowling hyenas and others of the carnivore which infested the region, lay rotting upon the ground. Anger was building in Barbizon as he surveyed the scene, examining each body with the idea he would find his wife. Then, from the mouth of Wopner came the terrible truth. "She has been taken by Ahmed Zam," said he, as he extended his bound arms and continued. "Unbind me, and for a price, the price of all these jewels, I shall take you where she is. I care not where I get my riches, from you or from him. Promise that I shall have these bags of jewels, and I will take you to him."

There was an intense rage overwhelming Barbizon, but Lynton placed her hand on his arm and said, "You have no choice my dear friend, as only he knows where we might find Leila."

Barbizon agreed to bury the treasure, and allow Wopner to return for it if his wife was safe, which Wopner assured him she was, as it was Ahmed's intention to sell her into slavery to a sheik in the Middle East. Barbizon leaned in close to him and said, "If she is not alive, neither will you be for long."

Wopner knew the treasure buried upon the site of the burned farm was infinitely more valuable than any ransom that would have been obtained, even to the avaricious mind of Ahmed Zam. He intended to kill Barbizon and Lynton if he got the chance. If not, he could have a thankful Ahmed do it for him with great glee.

Meanwhile, the band of raiders had reached their fortified camp, and there Ahmed Zam awaited the return of his confederate, Alan Wopner. During the long, rough journey, Leila had suffered more in anticipation of her impending fate than from the hardships of the road, and the other three women were quickly sent off with other men to be sold in the Congo.

Ahmed Zam had not deigned to acquaint her with his intentions regarding her future. She hoped she had been captured for ransom, for no great harm would befall her; but there was the chance, the horrid chance, that another fate awaited her. She had heard of many women, who had been sold into modern-day slavery by being taken north and then west through Namibia to be smuggled out on ships to the Middle East. The world was still filled with men who looked upon women as property and treated them as such.

She knew that as long as Barbizon and Lynton were alive, there was every reason to expect rescue. That Barbizon could find her she had not the slightest doubt. No spoor, however faint, could elude the keen vigilance of his senses. To him, the trail of the raiders would be as plain as the printed page of an open book.

Chapter 4

She Never Felt More Alive

Life is but a broken panel
Where anger can be shed
In evil's waterless channel
And the lean track overhead.

Many embrace greed's machinations,
With hearts as cold as polished sins.
And souls at hell's way-stations,
Love it where endless night begins.

Lynton Viñas was an astute observer of people, as was Barbizon. They felt that they needed to placate Wopner, but they gave instinctive looks to one another in recognition of the tenuous nature of their situation, realizing that after finding Leila, there would have to be a reckoning with Zam and Wopner. Lynton thought of how long it had been since she communicated with Wayne, and that, as always, he would be worried about her. He often joked that she was a headache he loved.

They walked into Zam's encampment to the weary eyes of the band of renegades, moving slowly forward as Wopner exhibited a new cockiness, since he knew he was no longer to fear Barbizon. Stupid as he was, he didn't realize that the little 5:2, 50 kilos dynamic dynamo could be just as deadly an adversary as Barbizon. In fact, she might be deadlier since her physical skills at fighting, which had been honed by years as a boxer, were often underestimated. You messed with this girl at your own peril.

Within the encampment, Wopner passed hurriedly toward the dark tent of Ahmed Zam. He rose as Wopner entered. His face showed surprise as he viewed the tattered apparel of the Frenchman, and he looked with a scowl at Lynton and Barbizon.

"What has happened?" he asked.

Wopner narrated all, save the little matter of the pouch of gems buried back at the farm. He did tell of the grand treasure buried far away in the valley where Barbizon had grand riches hidden in a cave. The evil Ahmed's eyes narrowed greedily as his henchman described the magnificence of the treasure, which now seemed even more palatable than selling beautiful women at top dollar into slavery.

"It will be a simple matter now to return and get it," said Ahmed.

Barbizon and Lynton stood silently as the two cretins conversed. As Ahmed ordered Lynton and Barbizon forward, he devilishly grinned at Lynton through rotted teeth, licking his lips and said, "This one I shall take for my pleasure. In fact, I shall have her and Leila both for my delight tonight."

Barbizon shouted, "Do not make the mistake of abusing either of the women."

Lynton defiantly said, "I shall tear your heart out, eat it and spit it in your face you pile of vulture excrement. I am not a woman to be messed with."

Ahmed laughed, looked at his loyal soldiers of mayhem and said, "You little bitch."

Lynton smiled and replied, "You'll see how much of a bitch, if you mess with me."

Barbizon looked at the back opening in the tent where he saw a giant cage just outside, and there in it was Leila. He motioned for Lynton to look, and she acknowledged what Barbizon has seen. She winked and said, "Now."

Barbizon, ignoring all the soldiers with guns, went straight for Wopner, who instantly sensed what was happening and scurried out the back of the tent with Barbizon in pursuit, as the dumfounded soldiers were confused about whom to help, because Lynton, faster than a speeding bullet, had leaped forward as Ahmed was sitting crossed legged and immediately wrapped her legs around his neck in a vice-like death grip. She looked over her left shoulder and told the soldiers, "Make a move and I snap his larynx and dispatch him to hell where he belongs."

Ahmed, gasping for breath, held out his two hands in a stopping motion whispering "Stop."

Lynton gripped him tighter, and said to the soldiers, "Guns on the ground or I snap his neck."

Barbizon entered the tent with Leila by his side. Looking at Lynton, he smiled, for he knew she had strong legs of steel from years of dancing, and therefore, had the ability to dispatch Ahmed with ease as she sat defiantly upon his neck. She looked down at him and winked with her beautiful right eye, as Barbizon and Leila picked up the weapons, emptied them and tossed them into the smouldering fire in the far corner of the tent.

Lynton said to Ahmed, as she squeezed just a little tighter so he could feel her womanliness through her shorts, "This is what you wanted stud, but not exactly the way you wanted it. She motioned for Barbizon to bind his hands behind his back, which he did. She released her grip, and as the soldiers stood helpless, they walked out with Ahmed, Barbizon holding a rifle to his head.

No one dared approach them for fear their leader would be dispatched.

Ahmed said, "Don't kill me. Don't."

Lynton said, "Not so tough now are you?"

He did not respond as they made their way to a Range Rover. The other cars were rendered useless when they fired bullets into the radiators. Barbizon, as Lynton got behind the wheel of the Range Rover, kept the gun at Ahmed's head, and he fully intended to pull the trigger as they pulled away, but Lynton floored the accelerator and the car lurched forward, making Barbizon's shot only graze Ahmed's head, who rolled to the ground and scrambled behind a car as his troops opened fire. They had no time to hesitate, so Lynton zoomed forward, leaving behind a trail of undulating dust, which obliterated the views of the troops, making it impossible to fire effectively at the three escapees.

Wopner appeared suddenly, lifting up the furious Ahmed who screamed, "You let this happen. You are responsible. I ought to kill you where you stand."

Wopner said, "I know where the treasure is," without informing him that there were two treasures, one buried at Barbizon's compound, and the other in the chambers near the white supremacist village that had been all but rendered unattainable by the earthquake. However, now with Barbizon on the run, it was feasible for Wopner to get Ahmed to pursue him, and when the opportunity presented itself to free himself from the clutches of Ahmed, so he could escape and return to Barbizon's farm, retrieve the buried treasure and make his way through Namibia to the coast, where he would catch a steamer for France and the grand life he wanted so desperately.

Ahmed Zam thought for a moment. The buried treasure was of much greater value than those who were roaring into the Karoo, but they needed to be pursued, because they would alert the authorities. He told Wopner that together they would pursue them, make sure they did not contact the authorities and then steal away with the immense wealth.

The pursuit was made easier when the Range Rover being driven by Lynton, while plying over the rough, inhospitable terrain like a lumbering elephant, experienced mechanical difficulty and sputtered to a stop, with the engine knocking and a giant plume of smoke rising into the humid air. Time was not in the three weary people's favour, as they could see in the distance, maybe ten kilometres behind them, the rising dust stirred up by a band of horse riders in pursuit. Barbizon pointed to part of the escarpment that was considerably lower than others and said, "I know that place. We can throw them off our trail. Come, follow me."

Quickly moving through the table-like top of the escarpment in a wide circle they came to a river at another point, drank and took to the scrub again as the pursuers were fast catching up on their swift horses that they would fortunately have to leave at the base of the escarpment.

Darkness was beginning to settle down upon the escarpment, as these three perfect physical specimens darted ever forward, knowing their pursuers were not far behind. They were near the white supremacist village now, so they needed to quiet themselves in order to avoid detection as it was Barbizon's intent to slowly make way at dark, to avoid detection, to the Plains of Morel, where they would then work their way back to the farm.

The three crossed the rear of the village, keeping always in the densest shadows. It required but a few minutes until they had made their way to the plains where they followed the old game trail toward the south, until there fell upon Barbizon's trained hearing the stealthy padding of a stalking beast behind them. The nearest tree gave them instant sanctuary, for they were all too wise in the ways of the Karoo to chance safety for a moment after discovering that they were being hunted.

Now, for readers too young to remember the abomination called apartheid that existed between 1948 and 1994 in South Africa, where the whites systematically denied Blacks and other minorities to which they refereed as Coloureds, the basic human rights due all people, we must digress here to understand about this unique place our three heroic sojourners had just skirted. In 1994, this evil was ended through negotiations which led to a multi-racial inclusive society that today functions in remarkable harmony, primarily due to the efforts of one of history's greatest humanitarians, Nelson Mandela, who was, of course, branded a terrorist by America, because he dared demand justice from white oppressors.

Despite this inclusiveness today, there are small pockets of whites who simply have not accepted the inclusiveness of modern South Africa. Some of those people have retreated into their own worlds, where white privilege is still maintained, and they live in a few areas where they have been able to systematically alienate themselves from the change the rest of the country has embraced.

The village skirted by our three intrepid defenders of justice, Verwoerd Township, named in honour of the architect of apartheid, Hendrik Verwoerd, is about to play a significant role in the unfolding scenario. It is here that a small band of people to whom we have been introduced earlier, cling to the notion that they are descendants from those who escaped the lost continent of Atlantis as it sank into the sea, and eventually made their way to the Karoo area, where they, after thousands of years as the only white people in South Africa intermarried with the Dutch settlers and joined the Afrikaans minority that ruled South Africa for so many years. They had fought against the British as Afrikaners during the Boar Wars, and never relinquished their belief that one day they would claim their hereditary place as rulers of all South Africa. To this ideal, the devoted followers of a woman named Ra, adhered with tenacity.

Ra, as priestess of this group, had for years led her small band of followers in the ritual human sacrifice she said was required by the God of Atlantis, Poseidon, who, himself, had been exiled to Greece with the God, Zeus. Now, it is, I know, somewhat incomprehensible to image a group of people actually believing this preposterous tale, but just look at the USA, where 33% of the people actually do not believe in evolution, 30% believe that Noah actually got two of every animal in the world on his ark or 40% do not believe in global warming, and it should be easy to comprehend that there are those people elsewhere who embrace the absurdities that trap the minds of the weak into a prison of ignorance. This was the case with far too many people in Verwoerd, and like so many elsewhere, they fell prey to the manipulation of a woman who appealed to their dark sides. Unfortunately, this is the way of a world, where so many people grasp for a meaning to life, when there really isn't any. It is just life.

Ra had used this ignorance to her advantage. She convinced her older followers, who longed for the privilege they had lost to pay homage to a God filled with anger. For the younger ones, who longed for the privilege their elders had taught them was the natural order of things as ordained by the great God Poseidon, who, himself, was white, it was a more difficult task, because their minds were more open. Still, there were the few younger ones who embraced the insanity of the supposed superiority of white genes.

Ra had managed to maintain tight control over about 50% of the 2000 people who called Verwoerd Township home. A large part of the population did not know or simply did not want to know about the abominable religious rites her group practiced, living their lives in denial of the evil amongst them. This, unfortunately, is the way of a world where evil is allowed to incubate and grow, because people refuse to take a stand against it.

Since 1994, these people had managed to stay isolated from the changes that made South Africa one of the world's most harmonious nations. However, as our heroes crouched in a tree high above the plains, waiting for nightfall in order to avoid discovery, Ra was making her way with some of her bravest followers toward a spot on the plains where they had seen vast amounts of dust arising, which meant someone was on their way to Verwoerd, and they wanted to make sure who it was and what their intentions were, so they moved cautiously in the twilight toward the rising dust.

Barbizon and Leila embraced on a branch to the right of Lynton, feeling once again the warmth of love that was still growing as they had only been together a short time. Lynton smiled at them and nodded her approval, turning her back to them in acknowledgement that they might want to get more intimate, for she knew the glories of love. For her, life had begun only 4 years before, when she had finally met the man of her dreams.

Lynton watched the descending sun, lost now in memories of the love that had embraced her only four years ago. There was a rhythmic percussion of sounds around her in the semi-arid Karoo. Her eyes steady to the horizon, face brightly aglow with the last orange rays before the coming twilight of the stars, a smile slowly creased across her succulent, puffy lips as she embraced thoughts of lying in her Wayne's arms, nuzzling in his loving embrace. There's was a May-December romance that had wrapped them both in the ecstasy of a love that had gradually overpowered them in the realization that they had gone through other relationships as nothing but preparation for what they had found in each others arms. They had known the misery of loves that ended when partners practiced betrayal of the foulest kind, but now they were both thankful for their pain, because without that pain they would not have found each other, found the light that led them out of the darkness that had engulfed them.

Lynton intently observed the line where the heavens touched the earth as she heard the soft sounds of lovemaking between Leila and Barbizon. Her wide, dark, exotic eyes observed the sun slowly sliding below the horizon. Glittering rays shot out from the orange fireball and danced in the coming darkness. There was such beauty here in the Karoo, the beauty of a still somewhat untamed wilderness that reminded her of how she felt untamed in Wayne's arms, wanting to be a wild, wanton woman of desire to kindle his passion. Tears formed in her eyes and a few dropped down her soft, brown cheeks as she longed for her husband, longed to hear him whisper those words she never got tired of hearing. "I love you. I love you."

She was crying now, although crying controllably so the lovers to her back could not hear her. The tears cascaded slowly as she visualized Wayne lying in his bed 10,000 kilometres away.

At her feet, as the incredibly intense darkness slowly and methodically engulfed her, she imaged leaping off with eagle wings and flying toward the sitting sun. The sky was now turning blood red, reminding her that she would have to endure hardship to once again rest in Wayne's arms. Scarlet now emblazoned the immense sky, painting it like the canvas before a skilled artist. As the night deepened, a firefly danced in merriment while below the canopy of darkness was inundated with undulating waves of sparkling, benign green embers under a now star-speckled sky. Oh, how she missed Wayne. How she longed to be like Leila, resting comfortably in the arms of the man she loved.

She listened intently to the few animals that were stirring below. The wild beasts that once roamed the mighty Karoo were fewer now, almost non-existent, as most were corralled into game preserves for the tourists to get a taste of what it might have been like before the white man, with his insatiable need to kill and bring back trophies to hang in dens, showed up to defile nature. However, within the Karoo, some panthers still roamed wild and free, and the immense one that had been in that chamber at the sacrificial altar was now roaming nearby, prowling in nocturnal pursuit of prey to satisfy its enormous appetitive.

Barbizon's keen sense of smell picked up the spores of the panther, and he put his index finger to his lips, indicating to both women that quiet would be prudent. Behind some thick scrub about 100 metres away, a vine moved. All eyes instantly centered upon the spot. There was no wind to stir the foliage in the depths of the Karoo. Again the vine moved. In the minds of the three, only the presence of a sinister and malevolent force could account for the phenomenon, as their eyes bored steadily into the screen of leaves upon the opposite side of the trail. Gradually a form took shape beyond them, a tawny form, grim and terrible, with yellow-green eyes glaring fearsomely across the narrow trail straight toward the tree where the three clung to the hope it would simply go away.

Suddenly, into the clearing below walked what was, no doubt, a scout from Ahmed Zam following their trail. They could have screamed, but why alert he who was intent on capturing them. The white robed pursuer approached. Across the trail from the three, the panther crouched for the spring, when suddenly his attention was attracted toward the horseman riding up from behind the scout. The massive panther turned its head in the direction of the rider as all in the tree observed spellbound at what was about to ensue. The scout turned to look back at his henchman, unmindful of the near presence of the great cat. On he came, his neck arched, chomping at the bit between his teeth. The beast's whole attention now seemed riveted upon the horseman. They were abreast the panther now, and still the brute did not spring. Could he be but waiting for them to pass before returning his attention to the original prey? At the same instant, the panther sprang from his place of concealment, full upon the walker and then the mounted man. The horse, with a shrill neigh of terror, shrank sideways and before the scout could fire his weapon the huge panther leaped upon him, slashing his throat with one thrust of his mighty paw. The panther left him lying there, went over to the still alive scout, bit his shoulder with his immense mouth and pulled his screaming feast into the shrub.

Barbizon signalled that they could not climb down, as they should wait until the panther had finished its meal, as it would, no doubt, come back for its other kill to bury it for a midnight snack. This was the way of the beasts in the wild, and the way of men in the city who never had enough of anything, especially money. They heard a horrible sucking sound behind the bushes, and finally the animal did return and dragged off its other kill.

Lynton, now growing weary of being chased said, "I am tired of running from those cretins."

Barbizon, smiling, thinking back on some of the books he had read by Wayne Frye where Lynton had battled evil, said, "But you don't have your famous high heels from hell to take into battle with you."

Lynton reached up and broke off a small twig and rubbing it on the branch, made it into a knife-like instrument and said, "This will do."

Barbizon said, "We stay here, and the column of miscreants will follow this trail in search of their scouts. We will wait for the last of the column to pass. We jump them and take their horses, ride to Vosburg and contact the authorities. Afterward, we go back to the farm, retrieve the jewels and give them to the Arori. Then, we must rebuild our home and bury those who fell before the evil of Ahmed Zam.

The three hid themselves above and waited. They did not have long to wait until all clothed in white habiliments, a long column of riders proceeded beneath them.

One moment the riders were laughing and talking together, and the next the last three were seized upon as the tree dwellers leaped from above, knocking the men off their horses, grabbed the reins and galloped into the night so fast, the few riders who managed to fire bullets at them were ineffectual due to distance and darkness.

Lynton felt a surge of intense energy, as now she was not confined to walking, but was atop a swift horse that galloped through the night, a virtual winged mount that almost seemed to take flight. She was filled with energy and once again on a grand adventure wrought with danger, but oh my, she never felt more alive!

Chapter 5

How Do You Kill the Living Dead

Voices of jackals calling
And, loud in the hush between,
A morsel of dry earth falling
From the flanks of the scarred ravine.

And the solemn firmament marches,
And the hosts of heaven rise
Framed through the iron arches,
Banded and barred by the ties.

They feel the far distance humming,
And they see the lights so plain,
And they know their pursuers are coming,
But onward they gallop, for it is life they claim.

Unfortunately, it was not just the pursuers from behind that they had to avoid. Barbizon could smell the spores of the white supremacists before them, as behind them the band led by Ahmed Zam and Allan Wopner galloped furiously.

The primitive instinct of self-preservation acknowledges many arts and wiles; as with Barbizon, the smell of death was equally prominent behind and before them. They were moving swiftly from one terror into the arms of another, but what choice had they? To their left was the escarpment edge rising almost straight up which presented an impregnable boundary from where they currently were, and to their right was a giant ravine waiting a few kilometres away where their escape would be halted or they could leap to their deaths into the rocks below. Vosburg was straight ahead, but between them and safety were Ra and her band of loyal adherents. Behind them was the evil of Ahmed Zam and Allan Wopner.

In a little moonlit glade ahead of them, the great hope for escape seemed blocked. The course they were taking would carry them directly into the religious zealots who worshipped a myth. Which were worse, religious zealots or a pack of graven thieves? Some choice.

There are incredibly strange things in the Karoo, unexplainable things that border on what might be termed the supernatural. So, it is at this point that our three wily adventurers came upon something that was not only amazing, but beyond belief for most people who will read this tale. As the raconteur sharing this adventure, I do not ask for belief, only understanding that I am sharing what has been related to me. Truth or fiction is immaterial, it is only shared here, because without it nothing else really makes sense, and all three of these people who experienced it swear that it happened just as I am relating it.

Inured to danger, with both sides closing in on them, Lynton took in every detail of the scene which lay within the range of her vision. She had depended on Barbizon's superior skills honed by being the descendent of a man raised by apes, a man who had been taught to live in harmony with nature, a man who had survived living a primitive lifestyle in a primitive area of South Africa, but now her instincts in regards to the supernatural were about to trump the skills of Barbizon.

As Lynton entertained frightful thoughts of what was about to befall them, she suddenly became conscious that, as they were galloping toward Vosburg, there was something off to their left in the scrub that was also apparently following them. She galloped beside Barbizon and whispered, "There is something to our left, something else that is shadowing us."

"I know," said Barbizon.

But first on earth, as Vampire is sent,
Thy corpse shall from its tomb be rent;
Then ghastly haunt the native place,
And suck the blood of all thy race;
There from thy daughter, sister, wife,
At midnight drain the stream of life;

Yet loathe the banquet which perforce
Must feed thy livid living corpse.
Thy victims, ere they yet expire,

Shall know the demon for their sire;
As cursing thee, thou cursing them,
Thy flowers are withered on the stem.

But one by one they must fall,
For you desire the blood of one and all.
Shall we now call you by evil name?
That word shall wrap thy heart in flame!
Yet thou must end thy task and mark
The neck's last tinge, the eye's last spark.

And the last glassy glance must view
Which freezes o'er its lifeless blue.
Then with unhallowed teeth shall tear
The bulging neck below the hair,
Of which, in life a lock when shorn
Affection's fondest pledge was worn.

But now is borne away by thee
The blood memorial of thy agony!
Yet with thy own best blood shall drip;

Thy gnashing teeth, and haggard lip;
Then stalking back to thy sullen grave,
You go while the living over dead rave.

Those who were ravaged in horror shrink away
From spectre more accursed than they.
Oh, into your lair you seek these three,
For it appears their blood will give you glee.
So, now the legend of the Karoo lay bare,
For you desire the dynamic dynamo so fair.

Lynton eased up between Barbizon and Leila and she whispered, "Who or what is it that trails us in the scrub?"

Barbizon said, "You wouldn't believe me if I told you."

"You are talking to a demon hunter. There is very little I do not give credence to, but, of course, I am a healthy sceptic."

Barbizon looked at Leila and said, "You tell her. Tell her of the undead-dead. Then, we'll see just how sceptical she really is."

"My dear Lynton," said Leila, as they trudged along, Barbizon keeping a keen eye to his left where they were being stalked, "I am going to tell you a story that happened in the midst of the dissipations attendant upon a Karoo winter, when there appeared at the various parties of a place called Calvinia, which is very near here, a tall, dark figure called Werner. He gazed upon the mirth around him at these parties, as if he could not participate therein. Apparently, the light laughter of the fair only attracted his attention that he might by a look quell it, and throw fear into those where he felt thoughtlessness reigned. Those who felt this sensation of awe could not explain whence it arose. Some attributed it to the dead grey eye, which, fixing upon an object's face did not seem to penetrate, and at one glance to pierce through to the inward workings of the heart; but fell upon the cheek with a leaden ray that weighed upon the skin it could not pass. His peculiarities caused him to be invited to every house; all wished to see him, and those who had been accustomed to excitement, now were pleased at having something in their presence capable of engaging their attention. In spite of the deadly hue of his face, which never gained a warmer tint, either from the blush of modesty, or from the strong emotion of passion, though its form and outline were beautiful, many of the female hunters after notoriety attempted to win his attentions, and gain, at least, some marks of what they might term affection. One woman, although married, threw herself in his way and did all she could to attract his notice, although in vain. The common adulteress could not influence even the guidance of his eyes, it was not that the female sex was indifferent to him, yet such was the apparent caution, with which he spoke to the virtuous wife and innocent daughter, that few knew he ever addressed himself to females. He had, however, the reputation of a winning tongue; and whether it was that it even overcame the dread of his singular character, or that they were moved by his apparent incredible charms that seemed to mesmerize the women, and also make men cower in his presence."

Barbizon interrupted Leila. "Don't be so dramatic, tell the tale and get it done."

"O.K., O.K., but I must do it chronologically with feeling and verve so she gets the true feeling for the horror that ensued."

"Barbizon, shaking his head, said, "O.K., do it your way, then."

She continued. "About the same time, there came to Calvinia a young gentleman of the name of Alec: he was an orphan left with an only sister in the possession of great wealth, by parents who died while he was yet in childhood. He was left to himself by guardians, who thought it their duty to take care of his fortune more than of him. This boy cultivated more his imagination than his judgment. He had, hence, that high romantic feeling of honour and candour, which was somewhat common among a few of the younger generation of the time. He thought that the dreams of poets were the realities of life. He was handsome, frank and rich. For these reasons, upon his entering into the high-toned circles, he put a gleam in young girls' eyes. Now, it was when he met the aforementioned Werner that some extraordinary things happened. He became acquainted with him, paying him attentions. It was thus that he asked his guardians for a bit of cash as he was not yet 21, so he could accompany Werner on trips about town. They willingly acquiesced."

Lynton, astute listener that she was, began to become engrossed by the tale, and listened intently as Leila continued. "Hitherto, Alec had no opportunity of studying Werner's character, and now he found that, with more of his actions exposed to his view, the results offered different conclusions from the apparent motives to his conduct. His companion was profuse in his liberality; the idle, the vagabond, and the beggar, received from his hand more than enough to relieve their immediate wants. There was one circumstance about the charity of Werner that was troubling though. All those upon whom his charitable nature was bestowed, inevitably found that there was a curse upon it, for they were all either disappeared or turned up dead, their necks being brutally assaulted by what appeared a vicious animal. At the town's casino and other gambling dens through which they passed, Alec was surprised at the apparent eagerness with which his companion sought the centres of all vice. There he entered into all the spirit of the games of chance. He bet, and always gambled with success, except where an occasionally more skilled gambler bested him, and then he lost even more than he gained; but it was always with the same unchanging face, with which he generally watched the society around him and seemed to always look at people's necks with an intense, almost hungering gaze. In every nearby town, he left the affluent youth, cursing, in the solitude of despair as to why he was so attracted to this man. Werner's elaborate carriage, as this was before the invention of cars, was similar to a funeral carriage, and amidst the various rich scenes of Vosburg, it was as if it always was the same, plying through the streets only during darkness, never seen during the day. Werner would set in it and stare out at people, mostly the poor, mostly blacks, and his eyes spoke more than his mouth. They were intense, foreboding and so piercing that the effect was to almost put individuals into a trance. Although Alec was near the object of his curiosity, he obtained no greater gratification from it than the constant excitement of vainly wishing to break that mystery, which to his exalted imagination began to assume the appearance of something supernatural."

Lynton, more curious now, felt a tinge of curiosity, because, as those of you who have read the book about her encounter with the vampire

(Aswang) in Tagaytay in the Philippines, she knows the power of those who prowl the night for victims of their blood lust. Leila continued her story. "So, Alec incessantly wondered about his new friend. One day he received two letters, which he opened with eager impatience; the first was from his sister, breathing nothing but affection; the other was from his guardians, as they encouraged him to be rid of his new friend, and urged, that this friend's character was dreadfully vicious, for that the possession of irresistible powers of seduction, rendered his licentious habits abominable for a young man to emulate. It had been discovered, that his contempt for the adulteress had not originated in hatred of her character; but that he had required, to enhance his gratification, that his victim, the partner of his guilt, should be hurled from the pinnacle of unsullied virtue, down to the lowest abyss of infamy and degradation: in fine, that all those females whom he had sought, apparently on account of their virtue, had, since his apparent disinterest, thrown even the mask of probity aside and publicly debased themselves by pursuing him relentlessly. This was particularly abysmal behaviour in the 1890's."

Leila took a deep breath and continued. "Alec determined, upon reflective thought, to invent some plausible pretext for abandoning him altogether, purposing, in the meanwhile, to watch him more closely, and to let no slight circumstances pass by unnoticed. He entered into the same nightly routine of carousing as had been the norm for months, but he became ever more observant of the abysmal behaviour exhibited by Werner. It became obvious to him in one instance that Werner was endeavouring to work upon the inexperience of the daughter of a lady who was interested in him. There was secretiveness to this whole affair, but Alec's eyes followed him in all his windings, and soon discovered that an assignation had been appointed, which would most likely end in the ruin of an innocent, though thoughtless girl. Losing no time, he visited the chateau of Werner one night to explore what his intentions were in regards to the young lady. Werner, when asked what his intentions were, said that they were as he supposed all would have upon such an occasion. He was interested in carnal desires."

Lynton was now grasping where all this was leading, but she elected to let Leila finish her story, which she did. "So, Alec was appalled and went directly to advise the young lady's mother of Werner's intentions. Telling her daughter to avoid Werner, the young lady was mortified and filled with anger toward her mother. The next day, her mother could not rouse her from sleep, and after banging on the locked door for awhile had one of her servants crawl around the back of the house and use a ladder to climb into the bedroom. What he found was shocking. She lay on the bed, body drained of blood and two small puncture marks in her neck, right at the jugular."

Alec had suspicions that the lady had been murdered, but the coroner's verdict was inconclusive, because the door was locked, and how could anyone get into the second floor room without the young lady screaming. Alec knew how. The person was admitted, because she knew who it was. Still, how did an intruder get into the room unless he used his own ladder, as the one used by the servants was securely locked in a storage shed, requiring a key from the butler?"

Barbizon displayed impatience with his wife as evidenced by the look of consternation on his face. Leila was ignoring him and continued. "Alec took some rooms downtown at a widow's estate and under the same roof as himself, existed a being, so beautiful and delicate, that she might have formed the model for a painter wishing to portray on canvass the promised hope of the faithful in paradise, save that her eyes spoke too much mind for anyone to think she could belong to those who had no souls. As she danced upon the plain, or tripped along the mountain's side, one would have thought the gazelle less agile. The light step of this girl named Irene was often in stride with Alec in his search for antiques, as he was an avid collector. Thus, his interest in the girl precluded his interest in Werner, but she did, one night, share with him a tale from her former home town of a vampire who had passed years amidst her friends by feeding upon the life of a lovely female to prolong his existence for months. This beautiful female, who once had a fetching figure, grew thinner and thinner, and several others, female and male, in the town told of feeling that they had been mesmerized by a strange man wearing a black cloak, having been in isolated places, where they would awaken hours later in a hazy condition, and upon examination later, notice that they had two puncture wounds in their jugulars. These troubling incidents were brought to the attention of the police, but after cursory investigations, nothing came of it."

You could tell that Barbizon had given up on interrupting, but his frustration with his wife's lengthening discourse was obvious as she continued. "Alec's blood would run cold while he outwardly laughed at such fantasies, but inwardly was aware of similar incidents that were occurring in Vosburg. In the process, Irene begged him not to be dismissive of her tale as some of her near relatives had been marked with the stamp of the fiend's appetite. She detailed to him the traditional appearance of this monster or maybe even monsters. This increased his horror as he kept reflecting on Werner. Still, he persisted in persuading her, that there could be no truth in her fears, though at the same time he wondered at the many coincidences which had all tended to excite a belief in the supernatural power of Werner."

Lynton, enthralled, interrupted. "And I believe you know of my involvement in a very similar incident in the resort town of Tagaytay in the Philippines?"

"Of course, we have read Wayne's book, and that is why we share this with you, because we are near the very area where the incidents happened, and the witching hour is among us now. You see, Alec began to attach himself more and more to Irene, who had won his heart with her sweet innocence. Irene though was not too aware of his growing love. However, when he told her he had to venture through this very forest, where we are now, after midnight to make a meeting in Springbok about 200 kilometres from here the next morning, she begged of him not to go after midnight through this forest. She described it as nothing more than a resort for vampires, a kind of, if you will, a place where they danced in the darkness of their abominations, celebrating their evil with nocturnal orgies. Alas, there was no swaying him, as he made light of it and bade her farewell, much to her chagrin."

Lynton had a dark, foreboding sense of where this was leading, but she continued to listen with a determined countenance. "The truth is," continued Leila, "he was concerned, but he was a man with steel nerves and refused to cower in fear. When he was about to depart, Irene came to the side of his horse, and earnestly begged of him to return, ere night allowed the power of these beings to be put in action. Again, he scoffed and proceeded onward. There came, as he approached this forest, the power of the a storm that raged with fury, and echoing thunders had scarcely an interval of rest as he made his way through the thick heavy rain among the canopying foliage, while the blue forked lightning seemed to fall and radiate at his very feet. Suddenly his horse took fright, and he was carried with dreadful rapidity through the entangled forest. The animal at last, through fatigue, stopped, and he found, by the glare of lightning, that he was in the neighbourhood of a hovel that hardly lifted itself up from the masses of dead leaves and brushwood which surrounded it. Dismounting, he approached, hoping to find someone to guide him to Springbok, or at least trusting to obtain shelter from the pelting of the storm. As he approached, the thunders, for a moment silent, allowed him to hear the dreadful shrieks of a woman mingling with the stifled, exultant mockery of a laugh. He was startled, but roused by the thunder which again rolled over his head, he, with a sudden effort, forced open the door of the hut. He found himself in utter darkness, the sound, however, guided him. He was apparently unperceived; for, though he called, still the sounds continued, and no notice was taken of him. He found himself in contact with someone, whom he immediately seized; to which a loud laugh succeeded; and he felt himself grappled by one whose strength seemed superhuman. Determined to sell his life as dearly as he could, he struggled; but it was in vain: he was lifted from his feet and hurled with enormous force against the ground. His enemy threw himself upon him, and kneeling upon his breast, had placed his hands upon his throat, and as the creature in a dark cloak was bending toward his neck with fanged teeth, people with torches were storming into the cottage. The evil creature, red eyes ablaze with indignation, instantly rose, and, leaving his prey, transformed into a huge black panther and dashed through the screaming crowd with their torches casting light on this thing from the depths of hell. The storm was now still; and Alec, incapable of moving, was soon aroused by 25 or 30 people who were frantically looking for a young girl. At the desire of Alec, they left him to search the other rooms for her. He was again left in darkness; but what was his horror, when the light of the torches once more burst upon him, to perceive the airy form of a fair-haired young girl of no more than 15; her lifeless form being carried by a grieving father, no doubt. Alec shut his eyes, hoping that it was but a vision arising from his disturbed imagination; but he again saw the same form being laid on a nearby sofa."

"There was no colour upon her cheek, not even upon her lips; yet there was a stillness about her face that seemed almost as attaching as the life that once dwelt there. Oh, but upon her neck and breast was blood, and upon her throat were the marks of teeth having opened the vein. All there hung their heads and whispered of the thing, the creature of the night, the shape-shifting vampire of the Karoo. Yes, this was more than just a vampire, this was a shape-shifting vampire that was able to take on the form of a panther to stalk its victims and satisfy an insatiable appetite for blood from the living."

Lynton, putting two and two together, was seeing exactly where this was leading, but she did want to hear the end of the tale, so she did not interrupt, as Leila continued. "Benumbed and stunned by the reality of what he had seen, he looked about at all the people who were in shock that they had not been able to save the child of one who lived in their village. They shared tales of an evil that had plagued their village now for nearly four months. They took Alec in tow, and proceeded with him back to the village a mere kilometre away. They were soon met by different parties who had been engaged in the search of her whom a mother had missed. Their lamentable cries, as they approached the city, forewarned the parent of some dreadful catastrophe. To describe their grief would be impossible; but when they ascertained the cause of their child's death, they looked at Alec and pointed to the corpse, indicating that this was the eighth victim in four months, and the authorities from Vosburg had simply ignored their pleas for help. After all, the town was run by whites who had no concern for the blacks who were not permitted to live in Vosburg, only allowed to work there during the day, and then forced to leave by midnight, walking many kilometres or taking a wagon filled with workers through the abominable forest where evil every bit as insidious as segregation dwelled."

"In this village, there was a man who frequented the place, buying jewels that had been recovered in nearby quarries. The next day, he arrived in the village, and to Alec's surprise, this man was none other than Werner, who placed himself in the same hotel as Alec and became his constant attendant. When Alec recovered from his delirium, he was horrified and startled at the sight of him whose image he now recognized from the eyes – the very eyes that had stared down at him in the cottage, and the stern, granite like chin below the mouth that was about to pierce his jugular with canine-like teeth in the darkness on that horrible night. Alec did not let on that he was now aware that he was staring at the shape-shifting vampire that was able to not only take on the traditional bat-like manifestation, but to turn itself into a huge, dark panther that could prowl about for victims, then shift back to human form in order to feast delightfully upon its prey, sucking the life from them in ghoulish delight."

The three halted at the insistence of Barbizon. He cautiously looked to his left, and said, "The stalker has been joined by another," be alert, for the time of attack may be near. He then held his horse's reins tightly as he said, "If we are attacked, do not tarry, do not wait for me. Ride as fast as possible for Vosburg and do not look back, never look back. What is stalking us is far more dangerous than Ahmed Zam and Ra."

Lynton, as they galloped on, encouraged Leila to continue her story, although she knew exactly where it was leading. Leila did so. "Alec recuperated nicely, sending Irene news of his delay. Alec perceived a change in Werner's demeanour, as his gaze seemed to be so very often fixed intently upon him, with a smile of malicious exultation playing upon his lips. The smile haunted him day and night, but he dare not broach his suspicions for fear of repercussions. During the last stage of his visit, Alec was intensely aware of how Werner disappeared during the day."

"He was only about at night, and his carriage driver could be seen outside the window, helping Werner into the dark carriage, closing the door and galloping off into the night, only to return and go to his room to rest throughout the entire following day. Slightly before sun-down, he would leave with Werner, only to return around sun-up with Werner in tow."

"During Alec's convalescence, he often dreamed of Irene, seeing her form in those infernal woods where he had come upon such evil. Irene's form would appear wandering amidst the woods with her back to him. Then, he would approach her, tap her on the shoulder and she would turn her pale face and wounded throat, with a meekly menacing smile upon her lips. Thus was the state of mind when he decided it was time to return to Vosburg and proclaim his love for Irene. He assumed he would be going back with Werner, but the man came to him in the dark of night, easing toward his bed and whispered, "I must go.""

"Reaching to turn up the oil lamp by his bed, Alec felt a cold hand stop him. This was the first time he had ever felt the skin of Werner, and it was as cold and hard as that of a corpse. He could see fanged teeth glistening in the moonlight that filtered in from the window to the left. He was about to render the elixir of life to this abomination. Just then, a knock at the door broke though the silence and Werner turned around, walked toward the door, looked back over his shoulder with those blood red eyes, said nothing, and opened the door to see Irene standing there. Again, he said nothing, just brushed by her and moved down the hallway rapidly. Irene went swiftly toward Alec, reaching down to embrace him as she knew that he had been close to being another victim of the terror of the night."

"As Alec struggled to get up, Irene helped him to the window, and they watched as Werner got into the coach and disappeared into the night, heading for those infernal woods where the girl had been killed."

"They then went down to Werner's room and broke in easily by using a hairpin from Irene. He related to her how Werner had only spent nights there, as days he always disappeared until the sun went down. Therein, they found he had left a few things, no doubt due to the haste to get out once Irene had interrupted his ghoulish pursuit of blood. Amongst other things, there was a case containing some earth. It was in a small box labelled – from Romania. Also, there was an obvious ceremonial dagger, with a few drops of blood on it. Telling Irene that he must investigate further, she reluctantly went back home, but urged him to only investigate in the day, and never enter those woods at night, which he willingly and wisely agreed to do, without reservation."

"He spent two days investigating the strange deaths of six girls and two young men. When he returned to Vosburg, he found Irene's parents were in distress, their daughter not being seen since her departure from the village when she had gone to meet Alec. His fear was that she had been intercepted by Werner, as she and the carriage carrying her and its driver had all disappeared. He became morose and silent; and his only occupation consisted in urging the constabulary to put more effort into the investigation."

"He could not feel interest about the frivolities of fashionable doings, and learning of his distraught nature, his sister arrived to comfort him. It was with her that his guardians decided on a grand ball to lift his spirits. The crowd was excessive. Alec was there with his sister, but did not have the heart to participate in the fun."

"He wandered outside on the veranda and stood by himself, staring into the darkness, contemplating the fate of Irene as he sensed someone behind him. He started to turn, but the voice said for him not to look behind him. The sinister voiced moved closer and whispered in his ear that Irene was going to slowly become a creature of the night, and that he should give up his quest to find her. He was filled with great trepidation. He stood stoically in fear as from behind a huge panther leaped over the veranda wall and bounded into the darkness."

"Thus, he breathed a sigh of relieve that he was still left breathing, obviously because the evil Werner feared discovery there and perhaps a mass manhunt that might lead the townsfolk to his lair. Alec went home that night and paced the room with hurried steps, and fixed his hands upon his head, as if he were afraid his thoughts were bursting from his brain. Evil was before him, and he knew not what to do. He roused himself; he could not believe that the dead walked, that some of the dead had become vampires, and some of those vampires could shape shift. He thought his imagination had conjured up the image his mind was resting upon. It was impossible that it could be real, but he knew it was. If before his mind had been absorbed by one subject, how much more completely was it engrossed now that the certainty of the monster's intentions preyed upon a mind of slowly unravelling dread. In his research of those who had disappeared without a trace; it had seemed that the dead were always less than stellar people, even the 15 year old girl was not very virtuous, as he learned she had blackmailed many of the men of the village with threats to accuse them of molestations, although there apparently had never been any such acts. But, surely there was nothing in Irene's background to indicate anything nefarious about her. However, he had made no threats to kill her, only turned her into a child of the night. The more he thought, the more he was bewildered. He thought of employing his own hand to free the world from such a wretch; but death, he remembered, had been already mocked by this evil creature that existed on the blood of the unsuspecting, the vulnerable, the easy prey. Anyway, how do you kill the living dead?"

Chapter 6

Alive But Dead

The dead are forgotten and lonely,
Where eternity has a dark shine.
Werner is not even a vampire only,
For he can shape shift in an evil line.

There are many mischief makers
Of the darkness out of reach,
Scurrying on their evil capers,
Sanity and hope to impeach.

The band behind our heroic three was gaining rapidly. So fast that it seemed the three felt their hot breathes upon their skin, but to their front the white cult of evil lead by Ra was also bearing down with speed. However, Lynton felt with each passing second that these were not the most fearful predators stalking them. What was hunkered down in the scrub to their left was a greater evil, for she began to sense that that predator was a familiar one, all too familiar.

"Tell me," pleaded Lynton to Leila, "more of how this tale has led to our present predicament."

"It is sad beyond compare, for now the evil shape shifter Alec knew had ensconced his beloved Irene and, no doubt drained her blood slowly, as a vampire does when it wants to make another vampire. Alec was in his bedroom one night talking to his sister when Werner appeared on the balcony outside his room. He motioned for the sister to come to him, and so mesmerized was she by his hypnotic power, she did so without resistance. When Alec moved toward him, Werner wrapped her in his cloak, shifted into a bat and flew away with her, and as he made way over the balcony, he dropped her viciously to the ground below. Screaming, Alec ran out of the room and downstairs to his sister's side. Alas, she was dead, and he was arrested the next day for murder, accused of throwing her off the balcony in a rage, despite his protestations that a vampire named Werner had killed her."

Lynton said, "And he was judged insane and spent the rest of his life in an asylum."

"Right, and the story I have told was found in the diary he kept at the asylum. All assumed it was the ravings of a lunatic, because the strange murders all stopped for a long time, nearly 100 years, and have only resumed in the past few years."

Lynton was in deep thought now, and she said, "He was gone for 100 years, travelling the world to find new victims to feed his insatiable need for blood."

Leila chimed in, "Perhaps. I have read Philippine tales of Aswangs, your version of vampires. Oh, but this Werner is the worst of the worst I believe."

"Yes, and he has returned to his old home," offered Barbizon, "and it is he and, no doubt, the mate he picked long ago, Irene, who, as panthers, are stalking us now in these woods that nobody dare enter at night, save us and our pursuers."

Ahmed Zam and Allan Wopner paused in the middle of the trail. Zam's keen eyes scanned every bush and tree within the radius of his vision. His tall figure presented a perfect target for the panther on the branch of the tree above. Ahmed looked upward just as the panther leaped upon him. He tumbled to the ground under its weight, as his comrades feared firing lest they hit him. No amount of firing could have saved him, for his throat was slashed instantly across the jugular by the largest panther anyone had ever seen.

All there suddenly realized this was not the only panther. From above, a smaller one leaped upon another man, slashing and growling as the two tumbled to the ground. Wopner and the others lashed their horses furiously and sped forward.

Barbizon, Leila and Lynton looked in dismay at one another as frightful screams reverberated through the forest. It was discernable that the panthers stalking them had turned, gone backward and attacked their pursuers from the rear.

The sounds of galloping horses meant their pursuers, fleeing the deadly shape-shifting panthers, were now nearly upon them. They skilfully skirted behind a grove of shrub trees, hiding from view as the group of frightened horseman sped by, Wopner in the lead. However, they got only a few hundred metres before they ran into Ra and her deadly devotees to the lost cause of Atlantis.

Our three heroes, to avoid detection, decided to sneak backward toward where the horrible screams of the dying were penetrating the darkness. Hiding in the thicket, they gazed upon a deplorable sight. The panthers were sucking blood from the necks of those left there wounded. They did not feast upon the dead, for their blood had died. They wanted the blood of the still living.

Where are the jewelled words that cut the sky like glittering swords? Souls of those lying there cried in terror as the two fervent blood suckers perched upon them, draining their blood.

Our three heroes dared not approach for fear of attack as the ground had been drenched with death, and those who had died instantly were far better off. The air became a channel of death as the few green leaves were splashed with the blood of the dozen or so who had suffered in the initial attack from above. Naught but the sucking sound could be heard as silence in the Karoo was observed by every beast as the dark demonic devouring continued unabated. No word was there, no song, no bell, not even the stirring of a breeze. Only the two insatiable panthers and the dead could be observed. Above, a pale moon cast an eerie glow as those with fangs in their jugulars were whispering their pain while others wailed in agony of wounds from the furious attack of the two beasts, and for those who waited, the terror was more pronounced, because they knew their time was coming. Then there was a breeze that blew gently through grass and grain along a smoking plain and an uneasy silence fell.

How strange are the hearts of those with purity. Our three heroes stared at one another with sympathy for those they saw falling victim to the horror, the very evil ones who had been pursuing them with nefarious intentions, but they knew exposure would put them at risk, so they hid from view. Then, within the midst of the horror, they saw a lily in bloom, glistening in the moonlight as if there was hope for sanity. Suddenly, a dark cloud eased in front of the moon, and it became so black there that they could see nothing before them, and the cries of agony fell from the precipice of despair. As the cloud slowly passed over the moon, when the darkness before them faded, a beautiful woman stood among the dead and dying there on the ground. Beside her was that huge panther, but the smaller one was now gone. There were stars in the sky seeming to hang on a green ray. Oh, the woman stood naked there in the glen and all about her the evil seemed magnified as she gazed upon the wounded and dead.

She drew her dark hair from her eyes as the big panther stood there, looking up at her. Oh my, but then she smiled in the shadowy moonlight. The smile crept across her lips slowly like soft snow as some wild dawn makes mist. Those teeth were fanged like a cobra's and she bent down and kissed the panther passionately. The panther was seemingly satiated now, calmed by the kiss. It was then that she walked toward one man lying there on the ground. He was not scared. He reached up toward her, almost pleading for her kiss of death. She kneeled and flung her white arms around his neck as the panther stood by her side. She was whispering something into his ear as she leaned over him, her full breast brushing his left arm. The words must have been mesmerizing, for he looked hypnotized. She had cast a vampire's spell upon the poor dying man. She gently bent over his neck and his eyes showed no fear. He was now embracing what was about to occur. He wanted to give her his blood, to give her the elixir of life.

She rose from her knees, her gleaming white teeth dripping with the blood from a willing giver. A silence among those on the ground spread as a intense large dark cloud again obliterated the moon. In the fading moonlight, she lifted her hands toward the sky, and the huge panther let out a mournful cry.

Lynton had seen vampires prowl about a place in the Philippines called Tagaytay, and she faced the evil of a thousand year old vampire called Ambragio with determination, but alas, this was an evil like she had never seen before in all her demon fighting. This female could shape-shift with eyes that were as dark as the blackest pit of a living hell. Her mouth curved with sweetness but contained poison.

Now, with the panther raising his head toward her, she swayed to and fro and into the darkness she gently seemed to embrace. The slight breeze appeared to be whispering something, as the three observers shivered from the cold.

Suddenly, the three heard from the female a sorrowful shrill. There was ill-will in the cry, as if she was harbouring dreadful things to come of red blood flowing from necks aflame. The cry reverberated about the nearby silent hills as if far off in cemeteries skeletons were dancing to evil's tune, and children cowered in sleep fearful of what would come beneath the full moon. The shrill cry faded as she turned and looked into the area where the three hid, her eyes ablaze. The whole forest suddenly, as another cloud covered the moon, was bathed in darkness as the sounds of the nearby battle between the forces of Wopner and Ra was filtered through in muffled agony.

The three heroes were no longer hidden, because as the cloud passed from covering the moon, now, there in the clearing before them stood a tall dark man by the woman's side. The panther had disappeared, or was this evil looking, mesmerizing man the shape-shifted incarnation of what had once been the panther?

The two incarnations before them looked directly at them with evil smiles. With voices darkly bent the vampires sent out a symphony of evil. The thin blood in our three heroes' veins flowed foretelling of vile, delirious pains to come. Suddenly, the clouds burst forth with what appeared blood red rains as the two bellowed in unison, "Who dies for us shall beautiful be as our bodies envelope them in the ecstasy of pain. All who defy us cursed shall be."

Then, looking directly at Lynton, who felt she had seen this man before, he said, "Ah, demon fighter, we were trailing you three for our feast, when a grand banquet appeared. Do not worry, we are satiated, our blood lust fully satisfied now, but I shall find you again, and how I will feast upon you, sucking the life from that little body, enjoying the grandeur of your warm red nourishment."

Again, a cloud covered the moon and darkness prevailed. When the moon emerged from behind a cloud, there before the three were two giant bats that flapped their wings in the stillness of the night as they darted away.

Like a sea of tumbling deaths, the three stood in awe at what they had witnessed. Their hearts rose and fell, shrunk and bowed. They knew their eyes had beheld two who were alive but dead!

Chapter 7

Trailed by Creatures of the Night

A tomb carved in coarsest stone,
A pillar with rank weeds o'ergrown,
Whereon can now be scarcely read
The verse that mourns the dead.

Point out the spot where Ahmed fell,
A victim in the vampire's dell,
As ever scorn'd forbidden wine,
Or prayed with face towards the shrine.

This vampire returned to his native land,
Making Ahmed and others die at his hand.
Yet died he as in arms he stood,
And was ravaged for his blood.

And blood lust quenched well
These two in harmony dwell.
Nor ear can hear, nor tongue can tell
The tortures of that inward hell!

But first, on earth as Vampire sent,
Thy corpse shall from its tomb be rent:
Then ghastly haunt thy native place,
And suck the blood of all thy race.

There along with your pitiful wife
Drain from people the stream of life;
Yet loathe the banquet which perforce
Must feed thy livid living corpse.

Those, upon which you dine,
Feed your evil you think divine.
People know not yet your accursed name,
But soon it will be written with a flame.

The blood from victims quenches thee,
And you revel in their pleading agony.
Oh, you do not let a morsel drip
From gnashing tooth and haggard lip.

Then, stalking to thy sullen grave,

Go with your wife to rave,

Till those in horror shrink away

From spectre more accursed than they!

While Lynton, Barbizon and Leila observed the ghoulish feast of blood, a protracted battle ensued between the survivors of the panther attack and the devotees of Ra. The fleeing horsemen fought furiously since they, unlike Ra's devotees, knew that what was behind them was more deadly than what lay ahead. They had seen the face of horror in those panthers that rose from the depths of hell.

Wopner managed to skip away in all the mayhem. Ahmed Zam's men finally surrendered, but it did no good as the victors slaughtered them mercilessly.

Ra's victory over the Muslims was obviously pleasing to those who had emerged triumphant as the superiority of the white race was actually proclaimed loudly by the bigots who could never quite come to terms with the fact that their way of life had been swept away by a new South Africa.

They were like so many others who simply could not face the reality of a world where whites were the minority and could no longer rule with impunity. It is strange, for example, that Africa and North America were not discovered until the white man showed up. Perhaps, the fact that non-whites were living there means it didn't exist until the whites found it. Subjugation was seemingly the natural instinct of whites toward non-whites.

While Ra and her followers were celebrating victory, Wopner was galloping toward Barbizon's farm and that treasure that meant more than life to him. The sparkle of gold trinkets blinds the eyes of those who see life as only rewarding when there are riches to fuel desire. Wopner imaged a château outside Paris, concubines, fine cars, grand banquets in the finest restaurants and abject aggrandizement from what would become his affluent friends in a grand life living at the pinnacle of a society where a person's worth is judged by wealth, not character.

Our three heroes sensed that they should make haste to the farm. They slipped past Ra and her modern Atlantis warriors, and galloped valiantly toward the farm, determined to get the treasure and turn to it over to the Arori as Bin Abi would have wanted.

Although her clothes were torn and her hair dishevelled, Lynton was a galloping vision of loveliness as she glided majestically across the Karoo plains, her breasts bouncing like two ripe melons moulded effortlessly on a thin frame that was seemingly sculptured by a skilled artisan of the female form. Her perfectly shaped legs, exposed to the very top of her thighs with flexing muscles that seemed to be dancing to the tune of a minstrel of magnificent merriment glistened in the rising sun that filtered through the parting clouds. There are some women who project a marvellous majesty no matter how much in disarray they might be. There are times when this writer must admit to complete awe when in her presence, because the magic she projects makes her the Houdini of happenstance in a world that responds to her elixir of effervescing efficiency of beauty that boils down to a simplified explanation that there beats within her a heart that knows no bounds in its demure dreaminess of delicious, divine diversity of exquisiteness. This is more than just a woman. She is the epitome of femininity in a form that says, "Mess with me at your own peril."

Meanwhile, Wopner had arrived at the burned out remains of Barbizon's tree house. He scurried rapidly to where the treasure was buried and so inured with the wealth he now possessed, had he not been fearful of the impending arrival of the three if they might have survived, he would have fondled the gold ingots with glee. He placed the treasure bags across the back of his horse and galloped away toward the Namibia border with eyes constantly glancing behind him to see if he was being followed. He saw dust and shivered!

As Lynton's eyes wandered across the Karoo, she shouted as she pointed in the direction of the dust flittering to their right, "I believe Wopner survived and that is he galloping toward the Namibian border."

"Yes," replied Barbizon, "and he, no doubt, looted the treasure." Then, he pointed to their rear, where great clouds of dust were rising far into the sky and continued, "But we have another problem at our heels. No doubt, Ra is aware that the treasure is supposed to be at the farm, and they ride to recover it."

Lynton said, "What do we do?"

"We ride like the devil after Wopner, and just hope they will not follow us, but all go to the farm. My guess is they will divide up, one group to the farm and one following us with evil intent, so we only have to deal with no more than 20 or 25 of them."

Lynton, managing a smile said, "Poor riders, we have them out numbered."

Barbizon chuckled as did Leila, and they galloped onward. Thus, they entered into the starkness of the Karoo desert now being trailed by about 20 to 25 riders, while the others headed for the farm and what they hoped would be the treasure. The three had no water and no food, and Wopner probably had stored up on water and some food at the farm. They were at a disadvantage, but their determination to save the Arori made them more determined than ever.

To the Karoo breed, time is usually a matter of a small moment, a haste free calculation, a commitment to survival in the harshness of the desert. There was no room for human error in an unforgiving environment.

As they galloped after Wopner, Lynton's mind reflected back on the encounter with the shape-shifting vampires, and she could not get it out of her mind that she had seen that man before. Yes, who was he? He was more than just the man so many people had talked of and feared. His name may have been Werner, but she knew he had another name, because she had somehow seen him before.

Vampires are mythological we are told, and Lynton was always a sceptic but what she had seen in Tagaytay years before when she was called in to battle against Ambragio and now what she had experienced in the Karoo, could not be denied. As she, with her companions, chased Wopner, she reflected back on the fears voiced by people in Vosburg and Calvinia. She wondered why there were no tales of vampire sightings in Verwoerd. Were white supremacists immune to these legends of blood suckers? Or, was there a reason why that shape-shifting giant panther had been in the sacrificial chamber? Perhaps, there was a connection?

Wopner was flaying his horse furiously with a whip, wearing him down with exhaustion, as he could see his pursuers were getting closer with the dust that ascended skyward. He was scared!

As Wopner approached the Namibian border, he knew that he must avoid the main, pot-holed, all-dirt road he was now paralleling at a distance of maybe 500 metres. There was an occasional vehicle that he sighted making its way to the border, and he wondered if he might perhaps get a driver to stop and with his trusty revolver in hand, commandeer the vehicle. No, because any one travelling the desolate road would probably be armed, and he might be outgunned. He would head toward the high mesa in the distance and try to sneak across the border on horseback.

Toward twilight, the three were within a few hundred metres of Wopner, but halted for awhile when they came upon a small pond. As they could now clearly see that Wopner had stopped high on the mesa, dismounting and looking to their rear, they realized that Ra's pursuers were within maybe five kilometres of them. They dismounted their horses and Barbizon, already almost naked, removed his loin cloth,and lifting his horse's hoofs one at a time he wrapped them with torn cloth. Nodding at the ladies, he shrugged his shoulders and pointed at their horses' hoofs, indicating that they should tear cloth from their clothing and do the same. What a strange sight it was to see a completely naked man, and two women in bras and panties walking their horses slowly across the mesa. This would have a duel effect; keep Wopner from seeing their dust from the horses' hoofs and prevent their pursuers from knowing where they were. Perhaps they could keep the 25 or so followers off the path they were following, and the one they sought could not see their dust and know how close they were.

As darkness descended upon them, they looked skyward and saw two giant bats winging overhead that swooped down on the far side of the mesa and disappeared from view. They edged forward for a few minutes, but they did not notice the four fierce eyes in the thick foliage to their right watching their activities with silent intensity and curiosity.

Thus, the three were almost upon Wopner now. Barbizon put his index finger to his lips indicating for complete silence as Lynton looked to her right and saw those eyes peering through the bush. She reached out and touched Barbizon's shoulder, and with her eyes signalled for him to look into the bush. He nodded affirmatively and whispered, "I know, we are trailed by creatures of the night."

Chapter 8

The Germ of Righteousness

There is a steel cold defiance
Searching for the dark core.
There is death's deep abyss,
Which whispers haunting tunes
Dancing on dead fingertips
And tasted upon dead lips.

Surrender to the unknown
With dark soul embracing it.
In a long, soulful evil kiss
Reach for the darkness of death
In the graveyard of cold tombs
Where a creature of the night looms.

The three saw the eyes of the menace stalking them again as the file of ebon horsemen behind the trail's bend riding slowly now in the wake of their leader was much closer than they thought, because they too had muffled their horses' hoofs to slip up on the unwary three, having left behind others to gallop with un-muffled hoofs to create a diversion.

Still, to their right were the menacing eyes glaring from behind the scrub. The three mounted their horses again and scurried quickly toward Wopner's position on the mesa, and the four piercing eyes did not move from their position. Lynton, as if she were afraid a loud voice might cause a catastrophe, whispered, "I even recognize those eyes. Those are the eyes of the man we saw before with the woman by his side. Still, I tell you that I have seen that man, seen those piercing eyes somewhere before."

A sense of impending danger seemed to hang like a black pall over the three. They were the only hope for the Arori to save their way of life, as the modern world only knew the power of money. Nothing else mattered in a world where the bottom line was the judge of all things. Lack of medical care, lack of shelter, lack of education, lack of even the water people drank was all traceable to resources being handed to corporations by governments for sale to the highest bidder.

As Ra's troops galloped cautiously forward, they were cognizant of eyes following them in the shrub. The baying of wild beasts was usually present as the nocturnal hunt for nourishment brought out the predators, but on this night, all was quiet, strangely quiet. Suddenly, the horses shrilled their neighs of terror as two giant panthers leaped upon the men so quickly they could not even fire a single shot.

In most battles, there is a good side and a bad side, but in this battle, both sides were bad. Yet, if this author had to pull for one side, it would be the shape-shifting panthers, because they were destroying the evil of white supremacy. Ra's men were throwbacks to a time when Africa was inundated with slave traders, who believed that the white man was superior, and thereby, had the right to subjugate those of a different colour. In fact, even the church, in those times, proclaimed that slavery was sanctioned by the Bible, which, of course, it was and still is if taken literally.

How does one effectively describe a battle between evil and evil? Is some evil worse than others? Is it always the choice between the lesser of two evils we must make? Do demons actually exist deep within us all that bring out the desire to destroy life? The 20 men scattered in overwhelming fear, some galloping back from whence they came, but they were the first to fall, as the panthers chased them and leaped on horse after horse to knock off the men, who were now on foot, franticly trying to escape the wrath of these two devils of darkness.

One soldier of Ra dropped to his knees and made the sign of the cross, for he knew exactly what these two creatures were. He knelt there making the sign of the cross with his two arms crossed; seeming to believe that the God whom he apparently assumed sanctioned racism and bigotry would protect him from these devils in search of blood. The giant panther seemed to be smiling and proclaiming, "You worship God and promote inhumanity you sanctimonious piece of cow dung. I spit upon your hypocrisy." Then with one swift swipe of its giant paw, the man's throat was slashed and blood spurted out like water from a geyser.

Lynton, Barbizon and Leila turned their horses and stopped behind a large group of scrub that rose at least 10 feet into the air. They observed the battle between man and beast dispassionately, for they had no sympathy with either side. It was then that Lynton remembered a story she had once heard about a man in World War I who said to a soldier, "Behold these hands and feet." And as the soldier looked down upon nail marks in the man's hands and feet, the man said, "Wounds like these were suffered for humanity."

The soldier threw his rifle aside. As it crashed to the pavement, he started to walk from the procession of marching soldiers but his commander said, "How dare you turn your back on your duty."

The soldier said, "I turn my back on war to serve a higher calling."

The commander took his side arm and shot him in the head and said, "We serve the cause of Jesus, but you answer to the devil."

So, it was on this day long ago that Lynton learned that in the grand scheme of things there is little difference between heaven and hell, between good and evil, between sanctity and non-sanctity. She saw religion as a method used to control people and make them do things in the name of God that would be abhorrent to any real God that might exist. She saw the evil of a society based on greed, and as she observed the panthers on a vicious kill rampage, she saw that as representative of capitalism, where the mighty ruled with impunity over those trapped in poverty. The vampires were no different than the capitalists. Vampires preyed upon the living for the blood that gave them eternal life. Capitalists sucked the blood out of the middle class and poor to feed their appetite for more and more, never being satisfied, always craving that next victim that would make them richer.

The panthers were oblivious to shot and shell. The aims of the frightened men were so poor they were now actually shooting each other. Ra and two other men by her side fell from their horses and moved without haste toward the three they had been trailing. Their compatriots were screaming, as they all wallowed wounded or dying on the ground. Then it began, the panthers moved methodically from one man to the other, first biting their jugular and then sucking with intensity to quench their thirst for the elixir of life offered by fresh blood. It was a feast of frenzy. They did not need all that blood, for it was required maybe no more than once a month to keep them breathing for all eternity, but this was like a fanciful frantic adventure they were on, because these people had failed to deliver the sacrifice in the chamber that day. These were those who had worshipped with a dedicated devotion that was fanatical, but now, having failed in their offering to the vampire, they were paying the price of non-obedience.

Ra and the two men stumbled before Barbizon, Lynton and Leila pleading for help. The three stared down at them and seeing a tall naked man and woman with fangs for teeth striding with evil intent their way, Lynton said with a smile, "You three should be aware these vampires like fruit, especially neck-tarines!" The three laughed and again Lynton looked into the eyes of the naked male. Their gazes met with intensity and she knew; she knew that she had seen him before, and he obviously knew her. Who was he?

The three turned their horses, and galloped away, ignoring the pleas of the three who were pounced upon by the two blood suckers. Their cries could be heard all about the mesa. Meanwhile, Wopner, despite intense fear from the screams he heard, slapped his horse incessantly, trying desperately to make the Namibian border.

J. Wayne Frye

As the three were getting nearer to Wopner, they looked skyward and saw two huge bats fly across the shadow of the moon.

The moon is full and shining
It fills us with delight
It is time we went hunting
We children of the night

Listen to us calling
The night is clear and still
And nature waits with bated breath
As we stalk down our kill

The sound of our wailing song
Will fill your pounding heart with dread
We come as bat, werewolf or panther
To take a victim from the street or a bed

The screaming of poor victims
Is sweet music to our ears
Beaten, bloodied and so raw

We laugh when you fill with fears

We take from you the sweet elixir
Sucking after the puncture bite
Rejoicing that you easily submit
To us, the children of the night

Come join in evil songs
We bay before the moon
As we perform life's ritual
And dance the devil's tune

We are Satan's dear children
Flapping in the moonlight
Delighting in the dark kingdom
We children of the night

The bats swooped down low and then arched upward toward a distant series of rocks, and there, on the moonlit mesa, the bats swooped downward again, almost as if pointing the way for the three to see there in the distance, a lone rider – Wopner.

He had raided the cave for even more treasure and was laden with gold ingots wrapped in a blanket on the back of his fast steed, headed for the Namibian border where he would follow the trail to safety on the coast where he would catch a steamer to France and a life of affluence.

The bats had no time to feast on Wopner, for the moon was disappearing now and the sun would come up. That was a death sentence for the children of the night.

As the three hurtled through the shrub, the discordant pounding sounds of Wopner's horse could be heard. They could see the border in the distance, but Wopner would have to veer off from a direct approach, for they would confiscate his treasure if he went through the official crossing.

Thus, did Wopner disappear on the far side of the mesa, galloping down a rocky hillside, with no dust showing his descent. Still, the three determined followers did not let up their pursuit, but when they arrived at the far side of the mesa there was no Wopner in sight as the area was dense with trees, a forest that covered his trail as there were two different routes off the mesa. Lynton said, "I'll take the left route, you two take the right."

Barbizon said, "But how will you stop him?"

Smiling, Lynton said, "Hey, I'm the dynamic dynamo."

Barbizon replied, "Be careful, and remember that he is dangerous."

As she galloped off, Lynton looked back and replied, "So am I."

Wide went Lynton's eyes in wonder and incredulity at how she had gotten to this point, as she beheld the galloping horse moving majestically forward with Wopner astride it. With parted lips, with heaving bosom, with anticipatory breath, the woman leaned forward, large-eyed, enthralled by the vision before her of a man with no soul, no compassion and no commitment to anything but his own greed.

She saw the sinewy form bobbing up and down and the bagged treasure across the horse's hind quarter. Not as an ordinary mortal might strike a blow did mighty Lynton Viñas shout at the top of her lungs, "You cretin, you murderer, you maniacal maniac of mayhem, get ready to die, because I am showing you no mercy, just as you showed no mercy to those you have killed."

Wopner could not help but laugh to himself, as he felt he had nothing to fear from a 5 foot 2 inch little Filipino girl. He was foolish!

Little did he know that he was courting death as these two in the silence of mingled joy and sorrow passed along through the forest, and as the night was waning with the moon now giving way to the sun, there came faintly to the brain of Lynton the knowledge that this was about to become an epic battle between her and Wopner. Strangely, she had no fear, because win, lose or draw, this was a woman who had been to the mountaintop of evil often, and when she faced it she did so with pure heart and a commitment to justice in a world where it did not exist for most people. She wondered about the vampires, and how, with daybreak approaching, they had pointed the way to Wopner. There was something strange about that and about the fact she knew that face.

As she now came within 100 metres of Wopner that naked man's face popped into her mind. He wanted to let her know where Wopner was, wanted him captured and his treasure used to help the Arori. Why? Why? Why? Why did a vampire have a heart? Why did an evil entity want to help Lynton? Deep in the soul of even an evil entity, perhaps lurked the germ of righteousness.

Chapter 9

Rage Against the Dying Light

And the monstrous heaven rejoices,

And the earth allows again,

Meetings, greetings, and voices

In this evil devil's den.

Two determined foes now face off.

The titanic battle must begin.

Never at the dynamic dynamo scoff,

Because she will see it through to the end.

Kipling wrote of a face-off between foes,

But it could have been no bolder than these two.

So, when the campfire blazes and glows,

Tales of this epic battle will be told to and fro.

Underestimating Lynton has been a mistake of a few, and all lived or died to regret it. Her body forged in long hours practicing dance and volleyball, this is a woman who stands at the apex of determination and willpower.

It is said that east is east and west is west and never the twain shall meet until earth and sky come to stand at God's great judgement seat. Lynton was born and bred in the near jungles of a small province in the Philippines, and her young life was spent on a farm working every day after school doing the labour of a large man, but she never complained and never saw a task that she would not tackle. When she moved to Manila with her parents at 12, she saw they were struggling to put food on the table, so she left to give them one less mouth to feet. Still, her determination would not bend before adversity and she never missed a day of school. She washed in a nearby stream and hawked vegetables every afternoon after school. Her entrepreneurship allowed her to help feed her siblings, for she felt, although her mother and father used poor judgement bringing many children into abject poverty, the children deserved a hand up, as the very church that insisted they be born, of course, turned its back once they were.

On the other hand, Wopner had been born into privilege, but squandered every opportunity, assuming by virtue of birth, as so many do who are born into affluence, that he should be handed the keys to success. However, when his father hit on hard times, and eventually committed suicide, Wopner had no choice but to seek employment, and he settled on work with a mining company in South Africa to avoid the shame of being seen as a poor person among his affluent friends. This belief in privilege had driven him to murder and to seek fortune the easy way. Working for success is not in the DNA of most who come from privilege. He was one of those who graduated college and went into daddy's company as a vice-president, propping his feet up on a desk and barking orders to the under-linings whom he looked upon with disdain and contempt. This is the way of the modern oligarchy formed by the 1% at the top of the economic ladder who embrace the notion of modern-day royalty based on economics.

Yet, this was a person who never wavered in his greed, never believed he was inferior, but rather had the firm belief that he was superior in all things, including his ability to stand against any foe. He had beaten up many in his duties at the corporation that hired him for his dispassionate manor, the corporate executive assuming he would instil fear in the men. And, he did.

These two titans of tenacity from dissimilar backgrounds had both forged a stubborn determination not to fail when forced into battle with any foe. So, just as Kipling said, "There is neither border, nor breed, nor birth when two strong people stand face to face, though they might come from the ends of the earth," these two were inevitably headed for conflict.

Wopner had raided the chamber where great treasure lay and engaged in subterfuge of the foulest kind. He put a trusty steed under him, and galloped into an adventure based on murder, kidnapping, mayhem and misdirection.

Upon his tail had been Barbizon and Lynton, but of the two, Lynton was the one least likely to superficially be judged as a determined pursuer of physical confrontation. Yet, her small frame and demure manner was only an exterior, and even within that exterior one could gaze into the eyes of determination, for this was a woman who exuded an almost surreal self-confidence, boldness of intent and dedication to justice. She never bowed before the altar of greed and self-indulgence, but rather, pursued life on a higher plain, the plain that made the words she once delivered before a peace conference ring about the lonely, foreboding Karoo as she galloped to her destiny: "We shall suffer no attachment to greed, no taste for the good-life, no love of the mundane to seduce us from our devotion to the cause of the oppressed, the downtrodden, the insulted and injured masses of our fellow men who must endure the constant struggle to make ends meet in a world where they have been pillared with disrespect and disdain."

The morning mist was gathering, and the distance between them was narrowing, slowly but surely making the confrontation between them inevitable, and they both knew it. They were both galloping at a furious pace now. There was rock to the left, and rock to the right, and low lean thorn between. The sun was above the horizon, and its rays bounced about the barren land as if it was a spotlight on the stage of the coming battle.

Her beautiful, long, silky hair flittered about with each up and down bounce on her sturdy steed. Her posterior moved slightly upward and downward with each gallop, accentuating her fine form in the pants that were snug around her hips. Her smooth, hairless, sinewy legs with taunt calves that flexed with each stride of the horse were like a Toulouse-Lautrec painting of Polynesian women, imbued with distinctness of character and sensuousness. Her breasts swayed in unison as if dancing to a Ravel symphony with pulsating kettle drums. This was a real woman!

With a determined will, she was furious now, and was within one hundred metres of her hunted quarry. Lynton shouted at him, "You think you are tough you murdering hell-hound. Let's see if you can ride like the devil you serve."

They rode as furious as a hurricane wind. Up and over parched terrain, Wopner's horse was sweating now as he whipped and whipped it with each stride. Lynton, on the other hand, took not up the whip but gave the horse freedom to prove its meddle without physical banging. She whispered to it softly as a butterfly winging about on the hot wind. She rode stately and determined as the low sun lit the morning sky, the huffs pounding profusely at the break of dawn.

Upon him now was Lynton and she came to his side, put out her right leg and pushed the horse with immense power, making it break stride and tumble upon the ground. Arising, Wopner, with pistol in hand as Lynton dismounted and stood unbowed, was bristling with anger.

Lynton leaped into the air and knocked the pistol from his hand with stiffened legs of steel. He tumbled backwards and she fell on her back at his feet with a thud. He stood and shouted as she got up to face him, "Twas but a gift I let you live as long as I did, bitch."

Staring at him, Lynton replied, "If I had raised my bridle-hand, as I have held it low, the jackals that flee so fast would have feasted on your carcass after I laid you low."

A murderous heart within an evil body, Wopner was now face to face with his fate. He had killed in haste at Chemco Mines a man whom he loathed, but this woman whom he confronted now had his respect, despite the need to kill her for his own survival. He looked at her with eyes ablaze, but could find no fault in her courage. He turned to his right where the pistol lay near the edge of a cliff that plunged 500 metres to the rock strewn canyon floor below. Suddenly, their eyes met and fury was about to be unleashed.

Wopner dived for the pistol, but as he did, Lynton leaped toward it, too. They met in a tangle of arms, hands, legs and feet, both desperately struggling for that which would give one the advantage and victory over death. Thus, a Thomasonian poem filtered though Lynton's mind.

Do not go gentle into that good night,
Old age should burn and rave at close of day;
Rage, rage against the dying of the light.

Though wise men at their end know dark is right,
Because their words had forked no lightning they
Do not go gentle into that good night.

Good men, the last wave by, crying how bright
Frail deeds might have danced in a green bay,
Rage, rage against the dying of the light.

Wild men who caught and sang the sun in flight,
And learn, too late, they grieved it on its way,

Do not go gentle into that good night.

Grave men, near death, see with blinding sight
Blind eyes could blaze like meteors and be gay,
Rage, rage against the dying of the light.

Curse, bless me with your fierce tears, I pray.
Do not go gentle into that good night.
Rage, rage against the dying of the light.

Chapter 10

Unanswered Riddle in the Plains of Time

Swift as a spirit hastening to its task

Of glory and of good, the sun sprang forth

Rejoicing in its splendour, and the mask

Of darkness fell from the awakened earth

As the dynamic dynamo lifted life's flask

To drink the elixir of soon to be mirth

Lynton's old boyfriend, with whom she lived for six years, could attest when he was caught in bed with another woman, to the fury of Lynton's left hook. As she and Wopner scooted along the ground trying to reach the gun, she instinctively crawled on top of him and as she rolled off, landed a left hook to his chin. The gun slithered through his hand and almost fell over the precipice of the cliff. The two were upright now and feigning another left hook, Lynton landed a solid right to the belly of Wopner, doubling him over in pain. She then raised her left leg and brought her foot into his chest, knocking him backwards.

As he expelled the last bit of choked air from his lungs, he managed to stand straight, eyes bulging with rage, and stared at his opponent. Wopner threw a roundhouse left, but the blow was ill-timed and the spry, nimble and smirking Lynton ducked under it. Before Wopner could even register the dodge, however, another body shot with extended leg, this one to his ribs, sent fresh ripples of pain through his torso, as the dynamic dynamo pivoted to the edge of the cliff, where Wopner assumed a mere head butt would suffice to tumble her into the rocks below. He lowered his head and charged. Lynton leaped up from the ground like a jack rabbit in a briar batch and she soared skyward with her legs spread, landing on his neck with her death grip firmly entrenched, forcing him to the ground. He laid there helpless as she was squeezing the life out of him, but he reached to his left and felt the pistol, gripped it and knew that a shot to the head was his only hope. Lynton saw it from the corner of her eye and immediately let lose her grip and leapt upright, standing over Wopner as she extended her right leg toward the gun and kicked it from his hand. It fell to the edge, and Wopner rolled toward it, hoping that he could end the battle with a well placed shot. He rolled too far. He rolled way too far. He rolled into oblivion below.

As Barbizon and Leila rode up, Lynton stood triumphant once again against evil. She took a deep breath, sighed as she pointed to the sack full of jewels and said, "Let the treasure of Omar Bin Abi do some good. Let us ride with great haste to the Arori."

And thus they did, riding gallantly and triumphantly to assist those sit upon by a cruel system that bows not to the citizens it is supposed to serve but to the corporations that have a stranglehold on the entire world. They had done their part now, and all that was left was for the lawyers, with compensation in hand, which is the price of justice in a greedy world, to do theirs.

Barbizon and Leila would rebuild their farm and start over, and as Lynton bade them adieu, heading back to Vosburg, where she would take the bus to Cape Town, she looked about the Karoo, which she had grown to love and wondered about something that had not been solved in all this adventure. Where were the panthers – the vampires of the Karoo that had, for some reason, assisted them in the pursuit of Wopner? Was this to be an unanswered riddle on the plains of time?

Chapter 11

After All, She is the Dynamic Dynamo

Lynton, more than a little lonely,

Thinking of Cape Town divine

Seeks sweet solace only,

In the warmth of love's sunshine.

Lynton's first notion was to contact Wayne and let him know she was alright. Strangely, he was not his usually chiding self, as once he heard of her harrowing affair he felt nothing but gratefulness that she was safe back in Cape Town. He instructed her to stay out of mischief until he returned in a week. Of course, he should have known better, because this is the dynamic dynamo, and although the reader might think the tale of vampires in the Karoo ended, the truth is it was not over. Bear with me, and I shall tell of how things did not end there with the two bats flittering away in the moonlight, but rather a new mystery was developing in a beautiful seaside community outside Cape Town called Camps Bay.

Lynton was resting by the pool when her friend Tamu came running out all flustered and excited, which she was used to, as that was Tamu and what made him so much fun to be around. He handed her a long note that was delivered to the hotel school to her attention, which made one wonder why it had been opened, but, of course, Tamu was Tamu, and he had very little decorum about him when it came to Lynton, thinking he was her protector, although it was he who probably needed protecting more than she. He said the note contained the practical only up to a point and then veered into the wildly fanciful, and only a true demon hunter could solve the problem scribed on the note. It read as follows:

Titus Coetzee, of Botha, Coetzee and Momberg, Solicitors and Barristers, Camps Bay,

Nov. 19th.

Subject: Vampires

Our client, Ms. Gloria Minnaar, of Memory Lane in Calvania, has made some inquiry to us in a communication concerning vampires in Camps Bay. Now, most people would laugh at this plea from her, and frankly we had a good chuckle too, but seeing as we now have in Cape Town a renowned demon hunter from the Philippines, we thought it prudent to contact you. As our firm specializes entirely upon the business-related matters, we have therefore recommended that she call upon you and lay what we consider a fanciful matter before you, since you are considered an expert in these matters. She shall contact you forthwith.

Faithfully yours,

Titus Coetzee- Senior Partner

Tamu, filled with excitement, said, "So, do I get to participate in this adventure? Please, please, I want to work with the dynamic dynamo, so that Wayne may some day write about me in one of his books about you."

"First," replied Lynton, "calm down my dear flighty little friend. Yes, you can be Watson to my

Holmes, but settle down, because this may not be as exciting as you think. Let's wait and talk to him first. Frankly, I have had my fill of vampires lately, and I am still a sceptic, despite having battled what was assumed to be vampires twice now. Let's look at this from a realistic point of view. Does it come within my purview? Maybe, maybe not, but anything is better than stagnation. You know me, I need excitement."

Then, she got up, and the sunlight glistened on her gorgeous body like it was a spotlight on the stage of beauty. Tamu was gay, so it had no effect on him, but the men and women at the pool were mesmerized by the perfection of a woman who seemed totally unconcerned about looks, so much so that it actually added to her beauty.

Her honey sweet lips had that just licked look that made them appear lace soft. She had a sculpted figure that looked as if an artist had sculpted it in the manner of Venus de Milo. Her arched eyebrows looked down on sweeping eyelashes. Her delicate, soft, brown skin reflected the rays of the sun as if the big red ball of fire was begging to lick her skin in its effervescence. As she walked away with Tamu, her silky, dark-brown hair that cascaded over delicate shoulders all the way to her waist, fluttered about in the mild breeze. She was poetry in motion.

As she passed a neighbour on the way to her condo, she gave him a knowing nod that lit up the hallway like an electric jolt with her megawatt smile. She slowly ran her bright red fingernails through her hair. Spools of it plunged around her perfectly shaped face that featured that flat Asian nose and piercing brown eyes that glistened with the feeling she was staring right into your soul. Long after she left the hallway and entered into her flat, there seemed an aroma of mint and cinnamon that lingered in the hallway, as the neighbour she had passed still stood there, breathing deeply, breathing the scent of the most extraordinary woman he had ever seen. Ah, if only he could have heard her sweet voice as she spoke in soft tones to Tamu. He would have fainted.

She leaned back and took down from the bookshelf a large volume book entitled, *Strange Tales of the Sea.* She read from a chapter toward the middle of the huge book, "*Voyage of the Gloria Minnaar,*"

Tamu said, "You mean a ship was named after her?"

Lynton replied, "No, the other way around is more likely. Yet, it is in this story that rumours of a vampire aboard circulated, and two passengers disappeared on the voyage, presumed to have fallen overboard and drowned. Do you believe in vampires, Tamu? Believe in walking corpses who can only be held in their grave by stakes driven through their hearts?"

"I do not know. There are things that cannot be explained. There are tales of mythical creatures all over the world. Perhaps some of those tales are based on fact."

"But surely," said Lynton, "vampires may not necessarily be a dead man or woman? A living person might have the habit of vampirism. I have read, for example, of people sucking blood in the belief it would forever keep them young looking. There have been many documented cases, even cults that practiced this macabre ritual. So, we can explore this case, but we must explore it with an open mind, with the complete realization there might be rational explanation for everything termed supernatural."

"Do you think that name Gloria Minnaar is fake?"

"It doesn't really matter. I am going to investigate, because I am bored without Wayne here. I need to stay busy while on vacation from school. You know Camps Bay, Tamu?

"I know it - had a boyfriend there for a few weeks. It is full of mostly modern homes but there are some old houses which are named after the men who built them centuries ago."

It was then that someone knocked on the door, and a messenger dropped off a letter from a Ms. Gloria Minnaar. It read as follows:

You have been recommended to me by my lawyers, but indeed the matter is so extraordinarily delicate that it is most difficult to discuss. It concerns a friend for whom I am acting. This gentleman married some five years ago a Romanian lady, the daughter of a Romanian merchant, who owned cargo ships. After a time his love may have cooled towards her and he may have come to regard their union as a mistake. He felt there were sides of her character materializing which he could never understand. This was painful as she was a loving a wife and absolutely devoted to him - the point which I will make plainer when we meet. Indeed, this note is merely to give you a general idea of the situation and to ascertain whether you would care to interest yourself in the matter. The lady began to show some curious traits quite alien to her ordinarily sweet and gentle disposition. The gentleman has been married twice and he had one son by the first wife. This boy was now ten, a very charming and affectionate youth, though unhappily injured through an accident in childhood. The wife was caught in the act of almost assaulting this poor lad in the most unprovoked way. She struck at him but missed as her husband interrupted her. This was a small matter, however, compared with her conduct to her own child, a dear girl just under one year of age. On one occasion about a month ago, this child had been left by its nurse for a few minutes. A loud cry from the baby, indicating great pain, called the nurse back. As she ran into the room she saw her employer, the lady, leaning over the baby and apparently biting her neck. There was a small wound in the neck from which a stream of blood had escaped. The nurse was so horrified that she wished to call the husband, but the lady implored her not to do so. No explanation was ever given and for the moment the matter was passed over. It left, however, a terrible impression upon the nurse's mind, and from that time she began to watch her mistress closely and to keep a closer guard upon the baby, whom she tenderly loved. It seemed to her that even as she watched the mother, so the mother watched her and that every time she was compelled to leave the baby alone the mother was waiting to get at it. Day and night the nurse watched the child, and day and night the silent, watchful mother seemed to be lying in wait as a panther waits for its prey. At last there came one dreadful day when the facts could no longer be concealed from the husband. The nurse's nerve had given way; she could stand the strain no longer, and she made a clean breast of it all to the man. To him it seemed as wild a tale as it may now seem to you. He told the nurse that she was dreaming, and that her suspicions were those of a lunatic. While they were talking, a sudden cry of pain was heard. Nurse and master rushed together to the nursery. Imagine his feelings, as he saw his wife rise from a kneeling position beside the baby bed and saw blood upon the child's exposed neck and upon the sheet. With a cry of horror, he turned his wife's face to the light and saw blood all around her lips. So the matter now stands. She is now confined to her room. There has been no explanation. Her husband knows and I know a little about vampirism, but when we heard you were now living in Cape Town, we knew the woman who took on the Tagaytay vampire might be our only hope to get to the bottom of this affair.

Will you see me? Will you use your great abilities in aiding a distraught and flustered husband? If so, please advise me at your earliest convenience, and I will arrange accommodations for you and anyone you want to bring along with you.

Yours faithfully,
Gloria Minnaar
27-022-795-3563

Lynton looked thoughtfully at Tamu and shook her head as she handed him the letter – "Please text her and say, we'll be glad to look into the matter."

Tamu, thrilled at the thought of working with Lynton shouted, "Yippee," as he frantically sent the text.

The next day, they were greeted at the Camps Bay Hawthorne Inn lounge by Ms. Minnaar promptly after the sun set. Ms. Minnaar was extremely tall for a woman, well over six feet. She had loose limbs and a fine turn of speed in her elongated, smooth gait. The athletic frame had taunt muscles, her flaxen hair was scanty and manly looking but neatly coiffured, and her shoulders were broad and erect. "Hullo, Ms. Viñas. It is a pleasure to meet someone so renowned."

Lynton pointed at Tamu, and made his chest stick out with pride when she said, "This is my associate, Tamu Thorndike."

The introductions over, Ms. Minnaar lumbered into a seat with some difficulty, as she was way too large for the small chair. As she sat uncomfortably, Lynton looked at the face with heavy makeup powder on it. As she gazed into the eyes, there was something unique about the woman, something that made Lynton think she might have met her somewhere before. Where or when she could not fathom.

"Ms. Viñas," said the seemingly uncomfortable woman, "I come to you most humbly, as my husband and I met the very nice Kruger family on board a cruise ship awhile back. We became great friends on the trip from Constanta, Romania to Cape Town, and as the saying so aptly goes, we were inseparable. I genuinely like this family. They were a bit unusual, of course, as like my wife and I, they preferred the night to the day, and we were often up all hours of the night, as we slept days. Now, we do not live here, as we are from the interior, but we do have a small cottage here up on the bluff, all to itself where we can enjoy a fabulous, expansive ocean view on weekends and vacations."

To Tamu's incredible surprise, Lynton said with what appeared true earnestness, "Yes, I know all that actually, you came here last May, according to the ship's manifest."

"Ah, that is why I wanted you to look into this matter. You are an astute investigator, who leaves no stone unturned, and, I am sure will get to the bottom of this baffling situation. I do not believe in vampires, but I do believe there is something strange going on in the Kruger home, and Mr. Hardy Kruger, at my urging has decided to bring you in on the case."

Tamu was amazed that Lynton had actually checked into a ship's manifest to locate the names of the people involved. She was indeed an astute investigator.

Lynton asked her, "And have you been to the police?"

"How," replied a sighing Minnaar, "could we do that. We have no proof of anything, only a hypothesis of some in the household, which frankly, I think is preposterous. I mean, come on. Who believes in vampires?"

Lynton replied, "You would be surprised."

It was almost 9:00 PM by the time they took Minnaar's old 1965 Rolls Royce, chauffeured by a tall, dark, skeleton-thin man with a beak-like nose. He kept looking in his rear-view mirror at Lynton and Tamu. Minnaar, sitting in the jump seat facing the two, said, "Do not mind Ferguson, he is a bit unsociable I am afraid, but a more loyal, devoted servant no man has ever had."

"No problem, we are not here to make friends, only to solve a perplexing mystery," offered Lynton as Tamu nodded in agreement.

As they entered the stately old mansion, they were greeted by Mr. Kruger himself. After going over the particulars with him, Lynton said, "Now sit here and pull yourself together and give me a few clear answers. I can assure you that I am very far from being at my wit's end, and that I am confident we shall find some solution. First of all, tell me what steps you have taken. Is your wife still near the children?"

"We had a dreadful scene. She is a most loving woman, Ms. Viñas. If ever a woman loved a man with all her heart and soul, she loves me. She was cut to the heart that I should have discovered this horrible, this incredible, secret. She would not even speak. She gave no answer to my reproaches, save to gaze at me with a sort of wild, despairing look in her eyes. Then she rushed to her room and locked herself in, refusing to share any details of her behaviour with me. Since then she has refused to see me. She has a maid, Della by name, a friend more than a servant. She takes her food to her."

"Then the child from whom you saw her sucking blood is in no immediate danger?"

A concerned Kruger replied, "No, the full-time nurse we have for the child has sworn that she will not leave it night or day. I can absolutely trust her. I am more uneasy about poor little Jake, my dear son from my first marriage, as he was nearly assaulted by her. You see, Jake is crippled or handicapped or whatever term is proper for today. He is but 10 years old, and he is dependent on me, totally dependent. He is capable of doing many things himself, but his left arm is atrophied and his right leg suffers from poor circulation with no cure. So, he also walks with a pronounced limp because of a twisted spine from a fall he took when he was 6."

"You say she assaulted him?"

"Yes, I walked in when she was grabbing him violently, shaking him and screaming at him," replied a visibly shaken Kruger as he continued, "He is the dearest, sweetest, most loving child imaginable. He also absolutely adores his new sister."

Lynton was a master at probing thought Tamu, as she said, "So, there are three servants, a chauffeur, a maid and the nurse in addition to you, your wife and two children?"

"Yes."

"I gather that you did not know your wife well at the time of your marriage?"

"I had only known her a few weeks."

"How long has this maid been with her?"

"Always, as far as I know. I mean she is almost 65, and was my wife's nurse maid way back when she was a child in the Transylvania province in Romania. She is a fine woman, a very fine woman indeed"

"I mean no disrespect to her Mr. Kruger, but the jails are actually full of fine people who simply made one fatal mistake."

"I understand your point, Ms. Viñas," offered Kruger.

"Call me Lynton please, and perhaps it would be advantageous if we stayed here in your home, if it isn't inconvenient."

"Of course not,"

Lynton sighed, looked about the room and said, "This unhappy lady, as I understand it, has appeared to assault both children - her own baby and your little son?"

"That is so."

"But the assaults on the two children took different forms? However, she was, in your opinion, going to beat your son in an unmerciful manner?"

"Beat, I would not say that. She was shaking him in an extremely violent manner and seemed ready to scream at him when I walked in. How far it would have gone I cannot say, but it looked frightful."

"Did she give you an explanation?"

"Actually, she seemed ready to do so, but she screamed at me that I would never believe her, and she ran to her room. She has abstained from all speech since then."

"You pay a great deal of attention to your son?"

"Yes, very much."

"Well, jealousy of another woman's child is not unknown among stepmothers. Is the lady jealous by nature?"

"I don't know. However, I have never seen any indication whatsoever. She always got along really well with my son, treated him nicely, but frankly, my dear son seems to harbour some resentment of her."

Lynton was intensive with her questioning as she continued. "The boy gave you no explanation of the assault?"

"No, he declared there was no reason. That was it. Never in the world could there be so devoted a son. My life is his life. He is absorbed in what I say or do."

"No doubt you and the boy were great comrades before this second marriage. You were thrown very close together, were you not when your first wife died?"

"Very much so."

And the boy, having so affectionate a nature,was

intensely devoted, no doubt, to the memory of his mother?"

"Most devoted."

"He would certainly seem to be a most interesting little lad. There is one other point about these assaults. Were the strange attacks upon the baby and the assault upon your son at the same period?"

"They were."

Lynton always formed provisional theories and waited for time or fuller knowledge to explore them. She was now prepared to ask the most pointed question yet. "So, you all think your wife may be a vampire. She comes from Transylvania, in Romania and, no doubt, you know the story of Dracula, and, if you read Wayne Frye's book, *Lynton and the Vampire at Tagaytay Manor*, you know there is also another rumoured vampire from Romania."

"I have read the book, yes. Who hasn't read it or seen the movie. The name is Ambragio."

"Well, I am afraid there are many, but if the members of this household have read it or seen the movie, as you have, and maybe your friend Gloria Minnaar here, perhaps your imaginations are running a bit wild."

"I just want the truth Lynton – the truth, no matter what it might be," offered Kruger.

"I fear that your friend, Ms. Minnaar here has given an exaggerated view of my scientific methods. However, I will only say at the present stage that your problem does not appear to me to be unsolvable. It is late, but if your wife is still up, perhaps we should talk with her."

"Of course."

Kruger led Lynton, Tamu and Gloria up the stairs to a long, foreboding hallway with worn carpet and a musky smell that seemed to whisper death in the ears. Tamu was feeling a cold chill start to work its way up his spine.

The ceilings were corrugated with heavy oaken beams, and the uneven floors sagged into sharp curves. There was one very large central room to their left and Lynton asked to see it. There was a huge old fashioned fireplace with an iron screen behind it dated 1870, where blazed and spluttered a splendid log fire. The room was well ornamented and to one side hung some ancient African utensils and weapons.

Lynton turned to Kruger. "You have explored most of Africa?"

"Yes, I have brought back many objects, some very fine examples of primitive culture."

A cocker spaniel lay in a wicket basket in the corner. It came slowly forward towards its master, walking with difficulty. Its hind legs moved irregularly and its tail was on the ground. It licked Kruger's hand.

"What is it, Lynton?" asked Kruger, noticing her interest.

"The dog - what's wrong with it?"

"You know, nobody knows, not even the vet. It is a sort of paralysis. Spinal meningitis, he thought. But it is passing. He'll be all right soon," he said as a shiver of assent passed through the drooping tail of the animal. The dog's mournful eyes passed from one of person to another.

Interested, Lynton asked, "Did it come on suddenly?"

"In a single night."

"How long ago?"

"It may have been two weeks ago."

"Very remarkable. Very suggestive."

Confused about her interest in a seemingly innocuous event, Kruger asked, "What do you see in this?"

"A confirmation of what I had already thought."

"What are you thinking, Lynton? It may be a mere intellectual puzzle to you, but it is life and death to me! My wife could be a potential murderer - my child in constant danger! Don't play with me, please. It is too serious."

Lynton, ignoring his pleas, surveyed the room and noticed a bevy of arrows hanging on the wall.

She said, "And those arrows, where are they from?"

The Cameroon. They were used by the Meandi tribe at the turn of the century - they are poison tipped."

Lynton smiled. "I fear that there is pain for you, Mr. Kruger, whatever the solution may be. I would spare you all I can. I cannot say more for the instant, but before I leave this house I hope I may have something definite."

Now, looking over at Gloria Minnaar, Kruger said, "You bring me this woman, and she is playing games."

Gloria in earnest, replied, "She never plays games. That is why I brought her here. She is the one hope you have to protect your family from harm. After all, she is the dynamic dynamo."

Chapter 12

Lynton Smiles

Roses are beautiful but have thorns.
Thus, do not accept things at face value.
The perilous path is laid with a smile,
And the light can dim and defile.

The sleeping serpent often walks in
Harmony with all those about.
The fox is wily and plays deceit's game,
While stoking the malcontent flame.

Lynton, ignoring Kruger's insults, resumed her examination of the curiosities upon the wall. Of course, they were hung too high for her to reach, but she looked over at a tall chair in the far corner, and a stack of books to the left of the chair.

Lynton looked over at Kruger and said, "We need to speak with your wife."

Lynton was introduced to her, but the lady just gave her a blank stare. Ever the diplomat, Lynton said, "We are sorry to disturb you. I know you have been ill, and I can understand why. You should talk to us, unburden yourself from the terrible secret you harbour."

She seemed to wander off into delirium. "A fiend! A fiend!" she shouted.

Lynton bent over and whispered to her, "I can help."

Again, Mrs. Kruger shouted in delirium. "No one can help. It is finished. All is destroyed."

Lynton pulled up a chair and sat by her side, leaning in and whispering softly in her left ear, "Your husband loves you dearly. He is deeply grieved about all this"

She now lowered her voice to a whisper and replied. "And I love him. That is why I dare not break his dear heart? That is how much I love him. He is full of grief, but he cannot understand."

"No," replied Lynton as she motioned the others to leave the room. "He cannot understand. But he can trust. Face him with the truth. Will you not share the truth with him?"

"No, no, I cannot forget those terrible words nor the look upon his face when he thought I was abusing his son. I will not talk to him. Go now. You can do nothing for me but tell him only one thing. I want my child. I have a right to my child. That is the only message I can send him."

She turned her face to the wall and would say no more, but Lynton was not through. "Do you know who travelled with you from Romania, a fellow Transylvanian, whom you knew to be a man named Werner, a man thought to be accursed with vampirism. They have brought me in, because I have experience dealing with vampires, or people who think they are vampires. This man Werner became your friend, and I know that as your friend, though he may suffer from vampirism, he has no evil designs upon this family. In fact, he is appalled that he might be considered the cause of this trouble. You befriended him on the ship, even after he and his wife had, from necessity, due to the long trip, sucked the blood from two victims and tossed them overboard. My guess is that you found out about them, but because of the budding friendship, you could not bring yourself to expose them. Fear not, neither will I expose them."

Lynton got up, left the room and walked back downstairs with those who had accompanied her.

"There," Lynton said with a sigh, "are extenuating circumstances in this whole affair. She then looked over at Gloria Minnaar, and knew for sure that she had seen this woman before. Looking directly at her, she continued. "There were vampires, or at least those who thought they were vampires on that ship with you. Of course, there is no vampire involved here. I know that now."

As her last word trailed off, into the room bounded Jake. He rushed forward and threw his arms round his father's neck with more love than anyone could imagine. "Oh, daddy," he cried, "I did not know that you were here, yet. I should have been here to meet you. Oh, I am so glad to see you!" Kruger gently disengaged himself from the embrace with some little show of embarrassment.

"Dear boy," he said, patting the blond head with tenderness. "I did not disturb you because of my company, Ms. Viñas and her friend Tamu, and, of course our friend, Ms. Minnaar.

"Is that Ms. Viñas, the very famous Filipino demon hunter?"

"Yes. You know of her?"

"Of course," replied the precocious little boy.

The youth looked at Lynton with a very penetrating, almost unfriendly gaze.

"What about your other child?" asked Lynton. "Might we make the acquaintance of the baby? She was not there when I saw your wife."

Kruger reached over, rang a bell and the maid came in. He asked her to bring the baby down. The boy then wondered off dragging his poor, deformed leg behind him, and bent over from the injured spine. Presently he returned, and behind him came the maid bearing in her arms a very beautiful child, dark-eyed, golden-haired, a true delight to behold. Kruger was obviously devoted to it, for he took it into his arms and fondled it most tenderly.

"Fancy anyone having the heart to hurt this little darling girl," he muttered as he glanced down at the small puncture marks still evident on the throat.

It was at this moment that Lynton developed intentness in her expression. Her face was contorted with some pain it seemed, and her eyes, which had glanced for a moment at father and child, were now fixed with eager curiosity upon something at the other side of the room on the wall. Then she smiled, and her eyes came back to the baby. On its chubby neck was those small puncture like wounds. Without speaking, she examined them with care.

Lynton walked over to Jake. "Do you like her, Jake, your sister I mean?"

His expressive face shadowed over like a dark cloud had ascended upon him, and he shook his head violently as he blurted out, "No, no I do not like her."

His father said, "Jake has very strong likes and dislikes and lets them be known."

The boy quickly walked to his father and hopped up on his lap, nestling his head upon his father's chest.

Kruger gently disengaged him. "Run away and play now."

He watched his son with loving eyes until he disappeared. "Now, Ms. Viñas," he continued when the boy was gone, "I really feel that I have brought you on a fool's errand, for what can you possibly do to solve what is an apparent attempt on my wife's part to destroy the happiness in this home?"

"Oh," replied Lynton. "Quiet to the contrary. This is no fool's errand. You see, intellectual deduction is confirmed point by point through observational analysis and by quite a number of independent incidents, then the subjective becomes objective and we can say confidently that we have reached a fairly rational conclusion. I had, in fact, reached it before we arrived but was seeking confirmation of my suspicions."

Lynton looked over at Gloria Minnaar, and thought to herself, despite her kindly nature that this was one grotesque woman. Then Lynton said, "I have arrived at a conclusion, but to affirm it, we need to see your wife again. May we?"

"Very well, whatever it takes to put this nightmare to rest."

Lynton said, "Oh, it will not be put to rest, but it will be understood."

As they entered the room, Mrs. Kruger had raised herself in the bed, but she held out her hand to stop her husband as he approached. He sank dejectedly into a nearby armchair, while Lynton seated herself beside Mrs. Kruger. She looked over at Kruger and said, "Let me first say what will ease your mind Mr. Kruger. Your wife is an incredible woman beyond compare. She loves you more than you could ever comprehend. She has sacrificed her well-being for you."

Kruger sat up straight in the chair, and said, "Poppycock, she just indicated how much she cares for me."

"Do not read too much into her desire to be away from you, because she fears if she gets too close that she will tell you everything and destroy you. Let me explain to you how I solved this case bit by bit. You see, I know who Ms. Minnaar really is, but that is not important now. You know who she is too. You have known all along that this person, this supposed vampire from Romania adopted a name from your ship. The ship's name all of you arrived on. The ship's name was The Gloria Minnaar, out of Romania."

Ms. Minnaar, standing in the far corner of the room, was focused on Lynton now, not taking her eyes off her in case an escape was called for.

Lynton looked sympathetically at a despondent Hardy Kruger. "In exposing the culprit here, I must wound you deeply Mr. Kruger, and it is a wound from which you and this family may not recover."

"Get on with it woman. Please."

Lynton, again looking at Ms. Minnaar, said, "I knew this was no vampire doing this from the very beginning. I have been battling a vampire; no, vampires, in the Karoo now for a week, and the strange thing is that these vampires never harmed an innocent person. In fact, I believe these vampires were protecting me and my two companions from harm. Oh yes, they gorged themselves on the blood of the victims, but the victims were all evil men. Now, you and your wife saw this good, too. My guess is that the two people killed on board the ship were bad individuals."

As she said that, a sense of recognition swept over Kruger's face as he nodded in the affirmative. He sighed and leaned back in his chair.

Then, Lynton looked at Mrs. Kruger, but directed her remarks to Mr. Kruger. "You had seen the lady rise from beside the child's crib with the blood upon her lips."

"I did."

"Did it not occur to you that a bleeding wound may be sucked for some other purpose than to draw the blood from it? Sometimes, poison is sucked from a wound."

"Poison!"

Lynton was now in full-on revelation mode. "My instinct felt the presence of those arrows upon the wall before my eyes ever saw them. If the child were pricked with one of those arrows dipped in poison from a hundred years ago, the effect could be fatal. You see, just a quick glance at Wikipedia on my cell-phone, and you learn that the Meandi Tribe in Cameroon used arrow poisons made from plants that contain cardiac glycosides from oleander and milkweeds. This toxic substance in a small body would mean death within a few minutes unless it was sucked out. And as for the dog, if one were to use such a poison, would one not try it first in order to see that it had not lost its power? I did not foresee the dog, but at least I understand him and he fitted into my reconstruction."

All there were in shock at the revelations. However, more was to come. "Now, Mrs. Kruger saw what happened. She feared such an attack. She saw it made and saved the child's life, and yet she shrank from telling you, Mr. Kruger, the truth, for she knew how you loved the boy and feared lest it break your heart."

Kruger jumped up and shouted, "Jake."

"I watched him as you fondled the child. His face was clearly reflected in the glass goblet on the table behind you, Mr. Kruger. I saw such jealousy, such cruel hatred, as I have seldom seen in a human face when the baby was brought in. It is the more painful because it is a distorted love, a maniacal exaggerated love for you, and possibly for his dead mother, which has prompted his action. His very soul is consumed with hatred for his sister, and the attention you give her."

Mrs. Kruger was sobbing, with her face buried in the pillows. The she lifted her head and turned to her husband. "How could I tell you? I felt the horror it would bring you."

He got up, raced over to the bed and embraced his wife, sobbing uncontrollably as they found that love had not died, only been enhanced from the tragedy.

Lynton got up and motioned for her companions to follow as husband and wife embraced; sobbing together over the love they still shared, and over worry about what would be done with the child who had attempted murder. Of course, Gloria Minnaar had disappeared from the room, as the balcony door was wide open. Lynton had seen her leave, and made no move to stop her.

As Tamu and Lynton strolled out into the night air, they decided to walk back down the hillside and catch a bus back into Cape Town. The moon was bright and the sky was clear. About half way down the hillside, they both looked up at the flickering stars and the moon that was full and bright. A huge bat flapping wings that reverberated all about the hillside flicked across the front of the moon. Lynton smiled.

Epilogue

Or is He

Walking to Cape Town, Lynton reflects.

But Werner still seeks to bite succulent necks,

Off in the Karoo, where darkness covers faces.

Werner laughs, having watched Lynton solve

What was one of her very toughest cases.

The bus let them off near Queen Victoria Street, and since it was 4:00 A.M., Tamu, as always, insisted on walking Lynton home. As they passed the National Library building, Tamu said, "Just one more thing bothers me Lynton. You said you recognized Gloria Minnaar, who obviously took her name from the ship. Who was she?"

"That was Werner, a person called the Karoo Vampire, in drag. Oh, and I now realize why I recognized him when he was watching after me, Barbizon and Leila in the Karoo. He is the vampire I thought was slain in Tagaytay, Philippines. His full name is Werner Ambragio – history's most evil vampire, or is he?"

**Don't Miss These
Exciting Lynton Adventures
For Teens and Adults From Fireside Books**
Lynton Curls Her Hair
Lynton Walks on Water
Lynton and the Vampire at Tagaytay Manor
Lynton Viñas and Beowulf Perez: Demon Fighters
Lynton's South African Adventure
Lynton Buys a Cell-Phone and Hears the Voice of Doom
Lynton and the Ghosts in the Mansion on Balete Drive
Lynton Viñas: Shadow in the Darkness
Pursuit (Adults Only)
Chablis and Lynton in the Room of Doom (Adults Only)
Lynton Viñas: Demon Fighter in Black and White (Adults)
**Also from Fireside, Wayne Frye's
Exciting Aaron Adams Series**
Fall From Apocalypse
Armageddon Now
The Girl Who Stirred up the Whirlwind
The Girl Who Motivated Murder Most Foul
The Girl Who Said Goodbye for the Last Time
White Meteors and the Ghost of Sue Ann McGee
Something Evil in the Darkness at Hopkins House
When Jesus Came to Jersey as the Son of Thunder
When Jesus Came to Canada to Lead an Indigenous Rebellion
Chablis Louis Chavez Thrillers
Chablis: Avenging Angel for the Forgotten
In the City of Lost Hope
Chablis and the Terrorist Who Resurrected the Spirit of Che
Pursuit
The Disappearance
First Nations Series
Hockey Mania and the Mystery of Nancy Running Elk (Fiction)
Points of Rebellion: Aboriginals Who Fought for Justice (Non-Fiction)
**And the Acclaimed Holocaust Sports Book
Called a Tour-de-Force During
NBC's 2014 Winter Olympics Coverage**
How Hockey Saved a Jew From the Holocaust